OUTRAGEOUS CLAIMS

One gentleman claimed Miss Willa Drake as his wife—though she never had said yes to him. To her horror, the Viscount Revis had caught her in a legal snare that society would accept, even if she did not.

Another gentleman claimed Willa would be his love whether she liked it or not. Sir Nigel Allerton produced a bundle of papers that clearly made it preferable for her to lose her honor rather than have her mother lose her mansion and her younger sister lose her hopes for happiness.

All of which left Willa with a set of most cruel choices. She could be a wife. She could be a mistress. She could be neither. Or, as was becoming fearfully likely, she would have to be both. . . .

Marriage by Consent

Marriage
by Consent

Elizabeth Hewitt

A SIGNET BOOK

NEW AMERICAN LIBRARY

A DIVISION OF PENGUIN BOOKS USA INC.

Copyright © 1985 by Mary Jeanne Abbott

All rights reserved

SIGNET TRADEMARK REG. U.S. PAT. OFF. AND FOREIGN COUNTRIES
REGISTERED TRADEMARK—MARCA REGISTRADA
HECHO EN DRESDEN, TN, U.S.A.

SIGNET, SIGNET CLASSIC, MENTOR, ONYX, PLUME, MERIDIAN
and NAL BOOKS are published by New American Library, a division of
Penguin Books USA Inc., 1633 Broadway, New York, New York 10019

First Printing, June, 1985

3   4   5   6   7   8   9   10   11

PRINTED IN THE UNITED STATES OF AMERICA

For Ellie Vander Meulen,
who planted the seed

Willa Drake sighed heavily, brushed aside a stray chestnut-colored curl that had fallen into her eyes, and put down her pen. "I know you cannot like the scheme, Mama," she said, "but it is the best solution that I can think of if you wish for us to go on as nearly as we did before Papa died."

Anne Drake, bereft of her husband of nearly thirty years for less than a twelvemonth, dabbed at dry eyes out of habit. "I do not see how you can call it a solution," she said pettishly. "It is more likely to be our ruin, or rather the capping of it, for after what your father so unfeelingly visited upon us, we are near enough to the state now."

Willa willed herself to forbearance. She was well aware that the marriage of her parents had been less than ideal, and it was only natural that she should grieve more for her father, to whom she had been very close, but it was all she could do to remember her filial duty when her mother animadverted upon her husband's treatment of her and her daughters. Sir Hammish Drake had often been unwise in his business dealings, but more often than not he had speculated to cover the extravagances of his very fashionable wife.

"That is hardly fair to Papa," Willa said patiently. "We

have this lovely house and the funds to maintain it if we are but prudent. It might have been very much worse."

"You would know best," her mother retorted, "since Sir Hammish saw fit to put everything into your hands. I shall never forget my humiliation when Mr. Sledge read the will."

And I was never so glad, Willa thought but had the respect and prudence not to say. It would be going too far to say that her mother was a hopeless spendthrift, but to Lady Anne's mind a new ball gown *was* more important than seeing to it that the butcher was paid.

Anne Drake was the daughter of one of the premier earls of the realm but she had married a mere baronet—a mésalliance by the standards of her family. Yet in the first flush of an overwhelming attraction that both had assumed to be everlasting love, economies had seemed a triviality and the practice of them never learned.

For thirty years Sir Hammish had successfully juggled his inadequate income and assets to give his wife and daughters a life in the grand style of the first circles of society, but in his death the truth was out. What was left to them in the funds and other investments was pathetically meager, and the small estate in Yorkshire, which had seldom been visited, had been sold in the first month after Sir Hammish's death to cover the greatest debt.

Willa had forgone her own dowry to meet many of the debts of the estate, but much of the dowry of her younger sister, Leonora, was secure and her mother's jointure had in any case been inviolable. They did still have the London house, and enough to keep it and themselves at least in a quiet style. No, Willa did not consider it ruin, but she could understand why her mother must deem it so.

When the foremost hostesses of the *ton* were being enumerated, the name of Lady Anne Drake was always near the top of the list. An invitation to a dinner or ball at

Drake House, some maintained, had more social cachet than a voucher for Almack's. This distinction was life and breath to the baronet's relict; to no longer find herself on an equal footing with Mrs. Drummond-Burrell or Lady Jersey would devastate her.

Willa could understand her mother, but she could not share her feelings. Bred to life in the highest circles, she could still regard the endless pursuit of all things fashionable as an empty existence. A quiet life would have been no hardship for her, but in addition to the difficult adjustment her mother would face, there was Leonora to think of as well.

Leonora had just been presented to the polite world when her first Season had been cut short by the untimely death of Sir Hammish. Leonora, always good-natured, had said she did not mind that now she would never have grand balls given in her honor or a list of the most-distinguished suitors to her hand and fortune, but Willa knew that by nature Leonora was more her mother's daughter—just as Willa herself was clearly the daughter of her father—and felt that she should have at the least one London Season to remember.

In only a few days they would be attending a ball given by Lord and Lady Sefton, not precisely coming out of mourning before the end of the prescribed period, for their participation at the ball would not extend beyond conversation with friends; but it *was* a coming out of sorts from their voluntary confinement and notice to their friends that they would soon be resuming their life in the *ton*.

How that was even to be thought of in their present circumstance Willa had little idea. After many pensive hours and several sleepless nights, she thought she might have hit upon a scheme, but if her mother was dead against it, she was not sure it would succeed.

Sir Hammish might not have been successful at his

investments, but as a man of letters he was a man of renown. He had been a published poet and essayist before reaching his majority, and great minds deferred to his superior intellect, with all the literary lions as anxious to receive an invitation to one of his informal Tuesday-afternoon gatherings as the fashionables were to be noticed by his wife.

Willa had no pretentions of emulating her father's genius, though she shared his taste for literature, history, and a simple life of scholarly reflection. He had imparted to her much of his learning and she was far more educated than most young women of her station. It occurred to her that capitalizing on her father's prestige and her own reputation as something of a bluestocking might well be the answer. If she was suited to no other occupation, surely she could at least pass her learning along. But Lady Anne was horrified by the idea.

"A school!" she said as if the word left a horrible taste in her mouth. Her netting box sat on a stool beside the sofa, but she had long since given up the pretense of work. She was intent on watching her elder daughter, so like her in appearance and unlike in character, adding up accounts in a large ledger book, and using the time to make known her opinions. "Why not a gaming hell, Willa?" she added sarcastically. "If we are to place ourselves beyond the pale, pray, why not enrich ourselves to the greatest extent?"

"We haven't the capital to begin a bank," Willa remarked dryly, and then added more gently, "A genteel tutoring of young ladies of the first quality for a few hours each day would hardly place us in the company of sharps and coal merchants, Mama."

"It is the daughters of coal merchants and every other variety of poisonous mushroom that your school would attract. Members of the *ton* see to it that their girls are taught at home by a proper governess, as you and your sister were. *We* do not send our daughters to schools."

The argument was overstated, but not without truth. Yet Willa would not admit to defeat before she had even begun. "Our class system is not so rigid, Mama. Lord Thune's eldest son has only just become betrothed to the daughter of Mr. Elgrim, one of the first bankers of the City, and all the world is proclaiming it an excellent match."

"All the world knows that Thune is all to pieces," the older woman retorted.

"So shall we be if we do not apply ourselves either to economy or to a means of increasing our income," Willa said sharply, at last beginning to lose her patience.

This evoked a loud moan from Lady Anne. "Oh, this will be the death of me, I am certain of it," she said in dramatic accents. "Though whether it will be due to the heartlessness of your father or your own folly, I cannot say." She placed one elegantly clad arm over her aching eyes and lay back on the sofa. The lachrymose attitude she struck cast a pall over the otherwise bright and cheerful morning room where they sat.

Willa knew that the best way to deal with her mother's posturing was to ignore it. She sighed again and turned back to the figures she had been going over before the interruption. Her own head was beginning to ache and she could not but wish that her mother would retire to her own apartments, for her silence was as disapproving and distracting as her voiced objections.

Willa had no intention, as her mother seemed to have, of trusting to a vague fate to bring them about again, and meant to go on with her plan for a school, at least until it proved infeasible. Lady Anne did have a plan of her own to offer, but it was as completely unacceptable to Willa as her plan was to her mother.

The practice of many of the best families of repairing

lost fortunes by expecting sons and daughters to marry to advantage was to Willa one of repugnance. When her mother had suggested it in a discreet way, Willa had replied roundly that she would as soon be as Harriet Wilson was, a courtesan and honest about it, for she considered it no better than selling herself. She would rather live in a mean cottage on nothing a year than do so, and she meant that neither should Leonora be sacrificed in such a way.

One of the lessons most earnestly instilled in her by her father was that she never marry without care, deliberation and as much assurance as possible for the happiness of her future. Sir Hammish was never bitter; he never blamed his wife for any unhappiness that their mismatching had brought to them, but he made it clear to his daughter that more than superficial attachment, more than worldly consideration was necessary when choosing one's mate for life. With the example of her parents before her, Willa was determined that the man she would marry would be exceptionally suited to her temperament, her personality, her ideals, and her aspirations, or she would never marry at all. She knew well that many women married and found not protection but a trap from which they could not escape. After marriage a woman all but became her husband's property; even the grounds on which she might divorce him were pathetically few while he could divorce her almost at will if he was willing to face the inevitable scandal. It would not happen to her, of that she was determined.

Willa cast a surreptitious glance at her mother, but that lady had not stirred and Willa supposed she had fallen asleep. This time when she sighed it was in quite a different way, for she knew that she was a sad disappointment to Lady Anne, who felt that learning in a woman was unnecessary and more of a detriment to her future than an asset. "Men dislike being shown to disadvantage," she had said to her daughter on countless occasions, but Willa would not compromise her character to feed another's vanity.

Yet, if Willa was not the toast of the town, neither was she without admirers. At three-and-twenty she had not yet wed, but she did not consider herself on the shelf; it was, after all, her choice, for she would never marry just to be married. Willa had tried on many occasions to explain her feelings to her mother, but Lady Anne regarded her as nearly freakish in her ideals. To her, the only respectable choice a woman had in life was to marry, quite literally for better or worse. Any woman who allowed herself to dwindle into spinsterhood or became a maiden aunt to a sibling's children was an outcast or not attractive enough to have caught the eye of any eligible man.

Willa's thoughts succeeded in dragging down her spirits even more. When a footman came to inquire whether or not they were at home to Lord Revis, a young man who had stood their friend through much of the difficult settling of Sir Hammish's estate, Willa quickly snatched at the diversion and told the servant to bring him to them at once.

Lady Anne, who was not asleep, sat up when the footman left them. "Willa, why did you deem it necessary to have him brought here?" she asked crossly. "The room is disordered, and frankly, so are you. Run to your room for a moment and see what you can do to tidy your hair."

"Adam won't care for such a thing, Mama, and neither do I."

Lady Anne sat up, smoothed the creases in her gown, and said with exasperation, "He is an attractive, fashionable man, with influence in high places, excellent connections, a respectable fortune, and a most pleasing address. The offhanded way that you are given to treating eligible young men is foolish. It is small wonder that your younger sister should be out before you are wed and will likely receive offers that have passed you by."

Willa was not hurt by this attack, as it was too commonplace, but she was surprised at its import. "You think I should make up to Lord Revis?" Her light laughter sounded. "Mama, of all the men I know, he is the least likely to make up to me. He *is* a man of distinction and fashion; nothing less than the daughter of an earl would suit him, I fancy."

Lady Anne pursed her lips. "Make up to indeed! I don't know how you come to speak with such vulgarity. No doubt it is your association with that Mr. Gordon, whom I cannot like. He smells of the stables, and being kind to him only encourages his pretensions toward your sister, which I cannot countenance."

"You mean you *will not* like him," Willa corrected. "He is an unexceptional young man who would suit Nora very well, I think; they are much alike in temperament and have a deal in common. And he does not smell of the stables; he is one of the finest horsemen in the country and hunts with the first packs, which ought to give him some credit even with you, Mama."

Lady Anne did not reply, though her expression said much, for at that moment Viscount Revis was ushered into the room. Her black looks quickly turned to a welcoming smile. "Adam, how very delightful to see you. We heard that you were in Sussex this past sennight and did not look to see you for a time."

"Merely a visit to my sister, who you know does not care for town life and seldom leaves her home or children," he replied, bowing over her hand in the old-fashioned way that he knew pleased her. "It was concluded with a bit of haste perhaps, for when I am away from my dear friends—

such as you, dear lady—for any length of time, I find I grow dispirited and foul-tempered."

"Wretched boy!" Lady Anne said, lightly tapping his wrist with her fingers. "I do not believe you. As if anyone could imagine you foul-tempered. I believe it is some fair charmer that returns you to town betimes."

He smiled in a slow way and shook his head. "Not that, but I shall confess that I am come to attend tomorrow night a dinner Mildmay and Ponsonby are giving for Brummell in payment of a debt. It promises to be an occasion I would not care to miss." Finally he turned to Willa and greeted her, saying, "Poring over accounts? That is too serious an occupation for such a lovely day."

In a lady of less consequence the sound that Lady Anne made would have been called a snort. "I am sure I have told her so, my dear boy. She should be spending her afternoon as her sister is, at the milliners, having a new bonnet made, but a poor mother's advice is seldom heeded."

Adam Revis responded with a small sympathetic sound, but while he sat on the sofa next to Lady Anne as she indicated, he cast a quick, quizzing glance toward Willa that made her think that the sympathy was for her.

Willa started to turn back to her work, but instead took a moment to study the viscount from beneath her lashes. Lord Revis enjoyed the world and making himself pleasing to all. He was very well liked, and if he did have enemies, his position in the *ton*, which was unassailable, made them hold any dislike to themselves.

He was certainly a very attractive man. Above average height, his well-made form had the natural grace of an athlete. His features were even, his hair dark brown, and his eyes, of a similar shade, could be expressive or shuttered by turns. He had a quick mind and a ready, though somewhat dry, wit. Willa liked him very well, though she thought him too concerned with fashion and society. When he looked or smiled at her in a certain way that he had, she could feel the stirring of a discomfiting response. He was a dangerously attractive man, this Adam Revis, and she did not underrate him.

He sat with negligent ease on the sofa beside her mother, appearing utterly rapt in her fluid monologue. He was not dressed in the extreme of fashion, but his cravat was tied with exquisite care, his coat looked as if it had taken two stout men to ease him into it, and his fashionable buff unmentionables fit him like a second skin.

She had even heard her bookish father once declare that Lord Revis would strip to advantage and was handy with his fives, which she took to be pugilistic cant. She had heard that Manton's Shooting Gallery had no target beyond his skill, that he was renowned as a whip and a member of the exclusive Four Horse Club. He was a Corinthian among Corinthians; handsome and rich enough to follow his pursuits. But Willa found little of this enamoring; she thought it a waste that he put so much energy into what she regarded as so unimportant.

Willa was so lost in her thoughts about him that she hardly realized she was now openly staring at him until she focused on the faintly mocking smile he directed toward her. A bit disconcerted, she turned her head away from him to hide the faint color that came into her cheeks. But she did not escape his notice.

"Do you really fancy being a schoolmistress, Willa?" he asked. "I must say I find it hard to place you in the role. All the schoolmistresses I have ever met were women of indeterminate years, little style, and much intellectual pretension. Fair lady, it will not do!"

Willa was glad for the teasing style of his question, for it allowed her to laugh away the confusion she felt at being caught out watching him. "And how many schoolmistresses have you met?" she queried archly. "Not many, I'll wager.

My own governess, Miss Grant, who was a schoolmistress in Bath before she came to us, was very pretty, never dowdy, and had to come up to Papa's stringent standards of education."

His smile and voice were languid. "The exception that proves the rule."

"Well, I mean to proceed with style," Willa assured him. "I shall take a page from your friend George Brummell's book and treat all applicants with such disinterest that they shall be certain of my exclusivity. I shall be very fashionable, I promise you."

He sighed regretfully. "But your mama is right, you know. It will not do."

The laugh left Willa's eyes and she turned more fully away from her writing desk to better take him on. "I think it will," she said with quiet assurance, and then ruined the effect by adding, "Why should it not?"

His voice was a soft drawl that suggested a hint of perpetual ennui, but his dark, slightly hooded eyes were alive and, to Willa's mind, gleamed challenge. He waved an airy hand about the elegantly appointed room, with its delicate spindle-legged furniture, damask hangings, and finely paned windows looking out onto Cavendish Square. "A school here?" he said with a mildly pained expression. "In the center of Cavendish Square? It is not to be thought of. The vulgar will buy tickets just to gape."

Lady Anne expanded her ample bosom with satisfaction. "I have said the very thing to her again and again. Perhaps your word will carry more weight."

"I am not so sanguine," he replied sadly. "I know Miss Drake to be a very determined woman."

Willa gave him her sweetest smile. "Is that another word for stubborn?" She knew he was quizzing her, but with her mother present, it was a sore subject. "If you mean that it will not be considered good *ton*, that has never been a consideration in my decision," she said loftily.

"But Lady Anne tells me that you do this to be able to afford to maintain your position in society," he said in a gentle way. "If society will disdain your action, it is a paradox, is it not?"

"This is *exactly* what I have said," Lady Anne said, almost chirruping in her excitement to be vindicated. "You may reason with her if you wish, but I fear she *is* her father's daughter and will have her way whatever the cost."

Willa bristled defensively. She addressed Adam but it was for her mother's benefit that she spoke. "It is Mama and Leonora who find it hard to give up living in society. For myself, I do not care for such things. They will not be part of the school, and if the world disapproves of me, they may do so with my great goodwill. In any case," she added more matter-of-factly, "I do not even know if a school will answer, but I know we must do something, Mama; if you wish Nora to have gowns by Madame Céleste, and entertaining, you know, is ruinously expensive."

"There is no point in asking people if you are not going to give them the best," Lady Anne said, sniffing. "Who would come again? It is an economy in the long run, you know."

Willa was not quite sure she followed her mother's logic, but she was saved having to answer by the entrance of her sister. The door to the morning room was cast open with abandon and Leonora Drake, her guinea-gold hair, diaphanous overdress, and lace shawl trailing after her, literally ran into the room.

Most of Leonora's actions were quick, and there was about her an ethereal quality that had gained for her in her abbreviated first Season the title "sprite." Leonora was flattered by this and not averse to playing the part. She affected gauzes, muslins, and laces in all but the most freezing temperatures to give herself the appearance of lightness, and when at home she frequently wore her long tresses unbound.

"Mama, *they* have arrived," Leonora exclaimed with the breathlessness that was not affected but natural to her.

Lady Anne had no trouble understanding her younger daughter. She clapped her hands together with a childish delight and said, "The gowns for Maria Sefton's ball? And a day early, how splendid. Madame Céleste has outdone herself." She turned to Revis. "I shall not stand upon ceremony with you, Adam; you must excuse me at once, for the gown must be tried to see if any alterations will be necessary and these must be done before Friday."

Adam bowed gracefully and stated that he quite understood and had in any case been on the point of leaving for an appointment in the City. Leonora flowed out of the room and her mother followed in a more conventional manner, but Willa remained in her seat before the desk.

"What of you, Willa?" Adam asked, standing near the door now but not making any motion to leave. "Don't you wish to try your gown for the ball? Surely you attend?"

"Oh, yes," she responded, "but I tried my gown a full three days ago. My dresses are not made by Madame Céleste; I prefer the needle of Mrs. Reilley. She is not as *à la mode*, but she quite agrees with me that my style is not at all suited to the ruffles and embroideries that abound in Madame Céleste's creations. And there is the added bonus that, she being less fashionable, her time is not as much in demand and her prices are quite reasonable."

"Virtues indeed!" He glanced away from her toward the open door. Were he the sort of man to ever appear ill at ease, Willa would have said his posture was uncertain. He looked back to her again and came a step nearer to her. "I have no wish to pry into a private matter, Willa," he said at length. "The comments I made about you opening a school were meant to be quizzing, but I would not be a friend to you if I did not tell you that, truly, I cannot like the scheme."

"Why not?"

"I do not think it would meet your needs." He sat down again in the chair nearest to her desk. "I don't know how far you have gone in your scheme, but I fear that the expenses—both financial and those more intangible which you profess to disdain—will not allow you an adequate profit."

Willa regarded him thoughtfully. She could not doubt his sincerity or his desire to be helpful. "I know it is not a perfect solution," she admitted, "but it is the only one I can think of that will answer the immediate needs."

"Really? I can think of another."

"What? I would take my oath that I have been over every possibility."

"Marriage," he said succinctly.

"You cannot be serious," she said with a surprised laugh. "You know me well enough to know that I would never marry for such a reason. I could never sell myself for a bit of comfort even for Nora and Mama."

"That is the tree without any bark on it," he commented. "Surely marriage need not be a purely business transaction?"

"What you are suggesting is."

"But you do not know what I am suggesting," he said with gentle complaint. "Is there no one toward whom you might feel, ah, warmer response? If there is and there is also a bit of ready for a marriage settlement, where is the harm in that?"

"There is none, I suppose," she agreed readily enough. "We are talking at cross purposes, I think. I would not marry with repairing our fortunes only in mind. When I marry, it will be for myriad reasons and with reasonable assurance that my future will be harmonious."

His sudden smile lit his eyes. "Is anyone ever assured of that?"

"Perhaps not entirely," she conceded, considering this seriously for a moment, "but there are circumstances where one can be assured of *un*happiness, and that is to marry for the wrong reasons."

"Such as filthy lucre? You greatly relieve my mind."

Willa smiled. She knew he was still quizzing her but she could not quite gauge his humor. "Do I? I can't think why."

He returned her smile broadly, and Willa discovered a small dimple in his right cheek that had gone undetected before. "Can't you? I fear I am doing this rather poorly, but you see, I have never done it before," he said apologetically. "Marry me, Willa, and I shall contrive—in my poor way—to make you as happy as is in my power. It will certainly solve your difficulties, though you will not allow that to be a consideration."

Willa was stunned. She was not often in the habit of displaying amazement, but she could not doubt that it showed clearly in her expression now.

Before she could answer, he said, with just the hint of dryness in his tone, "You did not expect this? I have been more subtle that I supposed. I thought I had, at least in a small way, prepared you."

"I have thought your attentions those of a friend," she said baldly. "I have never considered you in such a way."

There was no mistaking the aridness in his voice when he spoke this time. "I shall ascribe that to your delicacy of mind and console myself that your dear mother certainly has. Haven't you noticed how often—such as now—we are cast together, preferably *tête-à-tête*?"

As he spoke, Willa realized the truth of what he said,

and could not believe she had been so obtuse that she had not even understood her mother's hint this morning. Their intimacy as friends had grown since her father's death, though she had known him since her own first Season five years ago. She regarded him now as she was sure her mother and sister did also; a friend of the family. As such, she never thought anything of being with him unchaperoned. With the estate of her father thrust into her inexperienced hands and only Mr. Sledge to guide her, she was so grateful for his assistance that she had fallen into the habit of easily seeking his company for help with some new difficulty or as an ear for her grievances.

She was a little dismayed at her own stupidity and more than a little cross with her mother for not giving her something more substantial than a hint if she had known this was coming. "I suppose you spoke with Mama," she said. "Did she plan for Nora to come in and draw her off?"

"I shouldn't think so. I didn't know myself that I would say this today. You haven't answered me, you know," he said with gentle accusation.

Adam Revis did not have the reputation of being a cold fish, but he was always a cool hand. There was nothing in his tone or expression to make Willa think that he was in suspense waiting for her answer. She did not doubt that he had regard for her, as she did for him, but neither did she suppose that what he offered her was more than a marriage of convenience; she needed funds, it was time for him to set up his nursery and secure the succession.

Yet, when she still did not answer and he raised his heavy lids a bit to take her in more fully, she thought she saw there an unaccustomed intensity, a stillness and expectancy. She became aware of a similar emotion in herself. This was not the first proposal of marriage that she had ever received, but never before had she felt her pulse quicken.

An inner voice whose source she could not claim urged her to accept him. She admitted to liking him and to a physical attraction, but she knew at once, and not without some regret, that they would not suit. With a small, rueful sigh, she began, "You do me great honor, Adam, but—"

"You cannot accept my generous offer," he completed. "Yes, I knew that would be it. Shocking presumption, I know. May I ask why I am rejected? I had the vanity to think that you were not indifferent to me."

Instead of replying to his question, she responded with one of her own. "Why have you asked me, Adam? If you try to convince me that the picture of me adding up accounts struck you so that you formed an instant *tendre* for me, I shan't believe you."

"Even if it were true?" he asked with a sudden enigmatic smile.

Willa found his words and tone disconcerting, but she chose to treat them lightly. "Come, admit it, Adam," she said in a chivying way. "You said yourself that until ten minutes ago, you had no notion of asking me to marry you. I think you have been overcome with a fit of nobility, and though I thank you for coming so handily to my rescue, I give you fair warning that you have had a near escape. A less scrupulous woman would have snapped at your offer."

"So might a more conventional woman," he said with a small sigh. "I am quite sincere in my offer, Willa. And you are quite mistaken, I had certainly *thought* of it before ten minutes ago."

But Willa could not allow herself to take him seriously. It would be fatally easy to say yes, to lay all her burdens on his broad shoulders and obey the flutterings of desire he could evoke in her. But it would not do, and she knew it. He was a creature of the world she disdained; there was liking, yes, but harmony of spirit she thought impossible.

"You know as well as I that we would be mismatched," she chided. "I am so bookish, I would bore you in a twelvemonth, and you are so fashionable I would be exasperated in an equal time. Let us agree to be friends and you shall not mind that I waste my afternoons reading poetry and I shall not mind that you pass yours with no better occupation than gracing White's to show off your taste in cravats. As husband and wife we should find these disparities fuel for every disagreement."

He could not help laughing at this. "I am not so shallow, I hope," he protested, "and in any case, it is my coats that generally excite admiration."

Willa felt a little relief that he was at last taking her lead away from seriousness. She was fearful that her rejection would harm their friendship, which she would not at all wish to happen. "Then we are agreed. Instead of becoming husband and wife, we shall be friends."

He carelessly played with the ribbon of his quizzing glass. "The one does not necessarily preclude the other," he pointed out. "Do not be too hasty, dear Willa. I fancy half a dozen schoolroom misses might prove more exacerbating than my personal habits."

"Regard it as a favor that I refuse you. We are a ruinously expensive family, you know."

"I have no fear of it," he said, still in that vein, but then his voice took on a soberer cast again. "If you would trust me in this, Willa, I promise you I would never allow you to regret it."

Willa was astonished and dismayed that he should continue to exhort her. "Please do not press me, Adam. I . . . that is, if there is more to your offer than a wish to help me, I am sorry if I give you pain, but please believe me that I know we would not suit, and that I say so with real regret." She felt most awkward saying this to him, and to mask her confusion she turned back to the desk and closed the account book she had been writing in. "I had best go to Mama and admire her new gown," she said in a very different way. "I must be very rude to you and beg you to excuse me. No doubt we shall meet at the Seftons' on Friday, if not before." She rose and held out her hand to him in a deliberately distancing way.

"No doubt," he agreed amiably enough as he rose and accepted her hand. He did not bow over it, but held on to it for a moment. "Of course, I shall not press you, Willa," he said with his slow smile. "If you cannot like my offer, you cannot." His voice was very matter-of-fact, but once again Willa thought she saw in his eyes a greater depth than was in his words or tone.

She felt compelled to respond to it. "It is not that I cannot like it, but that I really believe us ill-suited to be more than friends."

An elusive smile played in his eyes. "Not even if I contrive to make you love me?" he said in a teasing way.

Willa felt an unaccustomed rush of shyness and dropped her eyes from his. He cupped his hand under her chin and raised her face to him. His lips just touched hers in a light, almost brotherly fashion. It was a shocking impertinence, but she scarcely heeded this in her concern for the quick, fluttering response in her breast.

He dropped his hand and stepped away from her, saying quite casually, "Until Friday, then." And with the briefest of bows, he left her.

2

If Willa did not allow herself to dwell on her response to Adam's swift kiss, she could not help thinking on his proposal. She did not, of course, tell her mother, for she knew that that lady would have considered her refusal of him an act of unforgivable folly.

But she did trust Leonora with the information and the younger girl said at once, "I should certainly have had him, if I were you. Just think what it would have meant, Willa. You would be a viscountess and mistress of your own establishment without having to ever worry about pinching pennies again. And I know you like Adam; I would not believe you if you said you did not."

"Of course I like him," Willa agreed, "but there are a great many other men that I like and I haven't any desire to marry one of them either."

Leonora sighed a bit wistfully. "I suppose you know what is best, but if nothing else, at least we should not have had to worry about turning the house into a common school."

"Oh, but I mean it to be quite uncommon, you know," Willa said swiftly, and then added more soberly, "Do you, too, dislike my scheme so much?"

"I can't lie to you, Willa," she said almost unhappily. "I

should hate it, I am certain. But if you do not wish to be Lady Revis, I expect I shall get used to it, and so shall Mama. Don't fret over us too much, dearest. However careless we may be of you, we both know how lucky we are that you are so sensible and willing to look after us."

Her words were meant to soothe, but they made Willa feel very spinsterish, and she had the lowering thought that if that was what the world thought of her, it was wonderful that Adam had ever proposed to her and most likely his proposal was the last she would receive.

But poor spirits were alien to Willa's nature, so if she suffered from occasional periods of melancholy, she would not nurture them and would determine only to look ahead.

Accordingly, she made an appointment with Mr. Sledge to discuss with him how she should go about beginning her school. Though it was customary for a man of business to visit his clients among the quality rather than have them come to him, Willa preferred it the other way, for she did not want to flaunt her scheme in front of her mother, who would only be upset by knowing that matters were going forward.

On the morning of the day she was to visit Mr. Sledge (which was also the Friday of the much-awaited Sefton ball), she and Leonora, as was often their custom, rode out to the park before breakfast. Both sisters were excellent horsewomen, though Leonora had the edge over her sister. The keeping of hacks, as well as Lady Anne's carriage horses, was a great drain on their slender income, but Willa knew Leonora's great love for horses and riding and could not deny her the pleasure, when so much had been lost to her since their father's death. She only hoped that the expense of starting the school would not immediately force the sale of the horses, for that would be an added blow to her sister's dislike of the plan.

Leonora and Willa preferred to ride in Green Park early

in the morning rather than in the more popular Hyde Park. It had the advantage of being generally devoid of members of the *ton* at this hour, and the sisters, who enjoyed a good gallop, would not be condemned as hoydens for indulging their pleasure.

Long before their horses began to lather, they returned to a more sedate trot, occasioned not only by sense but by the approach on the path ahead of them of two horsemen. As the men approached, they became recognizable: both were well known to the ladies. It was a little surprising to find them together, for the men were no more than acquaintances, but each had been encountered separately on similar rides on previous mornings.

As they approached, the elder of the two men sketched a bow from the back of his raking bay. "Good morning, ladies," he said, doffing his curly beaver with a deliberate flourish. "You are well met."

"Good morning, Nigel," Willa said with a welcoming smile, for she knew she would be glad enough of his company as the younger man, Mr. Gordon, to whom Lady Anne objected as a suitor for her younger daughter, came up to them and quickly turned his horse to fall in beside Leonora. It was not that he and Leonora were ever rude or excluded Willa, but their empathy for each other was so great, their conversation so fluid, that Willa always felt a bit of an intruder or, worse, a chaperone. Today she would have an admirer of her own to claim her attention. Sir Nigel Allerton obligingly followed Mr. Gordon's suit and brought his horse beside Willa's. The path would not permit riding four across, so Leonora and Stephen Gordon, their heads already together, at least figuratively speaking, started off again as soon as all the amenities had been exchanged, Willa and Sir Nigel fell in a little behind them.

Sir Nigel was a tall man with a knack for sitting his horse so that his height never seemed out of proportion to his mount. He was not much past forty, with dark-blond hair already peppered with gray, and keen, light-blue eyes, which frequently displayed a ready but rather sharp humor. He was on very familiar terms with the Drake family, for he was a particular friend of Lady Drake and had even enjoyed some favor from Sir Hammish, who on the whole was more condemning of the fashionables than was his elder daughter. Having known him from her nursery days, Willa was inclined to think of him in an avuncular way, but his manner toward her was frequently mildly flirtatious and of late his attentions had become almost particular at times. Willa did not precisely think of him as too old to be her suitor, but she could not think of him in that way and did what she could to gently discourage his attentions.

But today his company was welcome, and she had no notion that he would find a prosaic morning ride an atmosphere for dalliance. His presence gave Mr. Gordon and Leonora the opportunity to know each other better while she could look on without boredom or awkwardness.

Speaking what was on her mind, Willa cut into a compliment Sir Nigel was making about her habit, and said, "Don't you think they look well together? I know that is a stupid thing to say, for they are so well suited in so many ways that that just makes one more."

Sir Nigel raised sandy brows. "You are looking for a match there? I rather thought Lady Anne meant to look higher for Nora."

"The Earl of Seton had begun to show a bit of interest in Nora before we went into mourning, but he has called only a few times since out of courtesy, so it could not have amounted to much of an attachment. Stephen and Nora have so much in common, their love for horses and hunting, long walks, and visiting old churches and ruins, and they can spend hours rapt in conversations that I fear I find utterly insipid." Willa looked up at him and smiled. "You must not call me a matchmaking schemer. You know that I have very high standards for matrimony, which I apply to Nora as well as to myself, but I truly think them idealy suited, and though he is not an earl nor is his income a grand fortune, he is an eligible match."

"Your mama does not agree," he remarked. "But I think you know that."

"Yes, and it is the greatest pity. Leonora loves society and it is easy for Mama to convince her of the delights she would enjoy as a dashing young countess. But though Stephen could not provide for her in the grandest style, I think they could be enough in the world to satisfy Leonora, if not Mama."

Sir Nigel laughed softly. "I think I shall be prudent and not side with either you or your dear mama. I shall simply say, Yes, they do look well together."

Willa allowed him to cry craven with a brief smile and let her eyes follow the young couple again. Mr. Gordon was a handsome young man with dark-brown curls in the Byronic style and dark-gray eyes that seemed solemn but were belied by his pleasant, open manner. He was an excellent foil for Leonora's angelic fairness and they set each other off to perfection.

Stephen Gordon had become known to them only the previous year when he had been introduced to Leonora at Almack's, and it was clear that he was love-struck from the first. Leonora had been a reigning belle during her first, abbreviated Season and many young men had found much in her to admire, but few had Stephen's persistence. As the others, such as the illustrious Lord Seton, had expressed their condolences and then gradually drifted into the courts of other beauties, Stephen had continued to call, and Willa knew that it was only his fine sense of propriety

that kept him from seeking to pay his address to Leonora
before her period of mourning was ended.

That and the openly voiced objections of Lady Anne.
Willa did not think she had any real objections to Stephen,
but she did not mean for Leonora to throw herself away on
a mere commoner when she was certain a title could be
had with a little persistence.

Leonora was young and much under the influence of her
mother, who filled her head with notions of a grand match,
but Willa knew that Leonora grew fonder of Stephen each
day, and had hopes that Leonora's sense would overcome
her biddability.

Willa had almost forgot the presence of her escort, so
lost was she in her reflections, but he laughed again and
she turned to find him looking at her in an amused way.

"You *are* determined to play Cupid, I think," he said.
"Is there a hidden romantic in you, Willa? I hadn't thought
it."

"Goodness, no!" said Willa, startled at the idea. "I am
not the least bit romantical, it is just this matching that I
should like."

"You informed me once of your views on the married
estate. Exacting criteria, as I recall. But perhaps you cher-
ish a secret wish to be wooed in such a determined way,"
he added with what she thought was archness.

She glanced up at him sharply to ascertain any deeper
meaning, but his attention seemed more on the road than
on her and there was nothing overly serious in his expression. But Leonora and Stephen had moved some distance
ahead of them, which she could not like, for if Sir Nigel
was going to be in a flirtatious mood, she would as soon
not be so alone with him. She really did not know whether
there was any serious intent in his occasional attempts at
dalliance other than self-amusement, but above all things,

she did not wish to find herself the recipient of another unwanted declaration.

"I might find it diverting," she at last replied, "but not in the serious way a lover would wish. I think we had better catch up to Nora and Stephen," she added quickly. "It will not do for them to be too much alone, and Mama would never forgive me if I allowed my preference for Stephen to risk Nora's name in any way."

"If Mr. Gordon were a belted earl, she might not object so vociferously," Sir Nigel suggested dryly.

"Very possibly," Willa replied coolly, for she would not discuss her mother even with her mother's friend. She applied heels to her horse, but Sir Nigel reached across the breach between them and grabbed her horse's bridle just above the bit. Willa at once drew rein and turned to him with angry amazement at his impertinence.

He instantly withdrew his hand. "I beg your pardon, Willa, that was an ill-considered action, which you must put down to impulse," he said with a note of apology. "But you see, I have been trying to speak with you alone for some days now and always seem to be foiled in my attempt. You needn't fear for Nora's good name. We will always keep them in sight and I am persuaded that Mr. Gordon is the sort that would always keep the line."

Willa was filled with an instant foreboding that he did indeed mean to declare himself. "Just the same," she said hastily, about to go on again, "I would feel better if we stayed with them. Return with us to the house, if you wish, Nigel, and we may talk then."

"But not alone, I fear," he said. "This is not a matter for company."

Willa's heart sank; there was that in his voice that told her that he would speak his mind. If she put him off today, he would contrive a means for tomorrow. Repressing a sigh that would have been rude, she started along the path again, but at a sedate walk and said dampeningly, "As you wish, Nigel. But I do hope it will not take long, for I think it will soon be time for breakfast and Nora and I should return to the house." And if that bit of flat unromanticism did not put him off, she did not know what would, short of the bald statement that she had no wish to receive an offer from him, which she certainly could not do, because it would have been both inexcusably ill-bred and presumptuous.

But Sir Nigel seemed neither put off nor in any hurry to come to his point. Instead, he engaged her in more of the flirtatious banter that she was in no humor to parry and pretty compliments that served only to increase her impatience for him to get on with it.

When he remarked on the rare loveliness of her eyes, she said in a flat, ungracious way, "Yes, gray is held to be an uncommon color I have heard."

His expression was amused, but not his eyes. "I was thinking of their fine speaking quality, not their color, though I hold them to be more blue than gray and most attracting." He paused for a moment and then said, "I know my moment is not best chosen, but the truth is, now that you are so nearly out of mourning and will be going into society again, I could contain myself no longer. You must know how much I have come to admire you, especially in the last several months as I have watched you be a source of spirit and strength to your mother and sister. How proud and strong you are become; there is a dignity about you which is tantalizing. It is only respect for your mourning that has silenced me any time this past month."

He followed this with declarations of love and desire, and with lowered eyes Willa listened and she did not even pull away from him when he reached toward her again and placed a hand lightly on her arm. But her listening was imperfect, for through her mind she played what she would say to him to give him least pain when she refused, as she must; so it was several minutes before she realized that she was indeed presuming his intentions. She abruptly removed his hand from her and again drew rein, forcing him to do the same.

"You must be more clear, sir," she said frigidly. "I am not certain that I understand you."

His mobile brows shot up. "No? I thought I was quite clear. I have told you that I find you the most attractive, most desirable woman I have ever known. I fear I shall never again know peace until you are mine."

"Pretty words, Nigel," she said aridly, "but be more precise in your import."

"I want you, Willa—more, I need you."

"How?"

"How? Do you mean how much? What more can I say to you?"

"I mean, in what way? But it does not signify; I think I do understand you. We must both be disappointed in this interview, for we have been quite mistaken in each other's character. I collect that making me yours does not include the formality of a ceremony." The look she bestowed on him was withering. "I would have supposed that your friendship with my mother, if no other consideration, would have protected me from such insult at your hands."

Sir Nigel gave no appearance of being abashed by her response. "Would you wish for marriage, Willa? You have made no secret of the fact that you believe marriage more a trap for most women than a protection. What I am offering you would be all of the latter and none of the former. Your dear mother has confided in me that all is not well with you financially, a delicate dilemma with no obvious solution. If you come to me, concern for money need never again be a consideration. If it is your reputation you fear, I promise you that I shall be all discretion. Not even your mother or sister need know of our connection. Simply trust all to me."

Willa sat her horse bolt upright, her very rigidity a reproach. She could scarcely credit her ears. It was not surprising, she supposed, that he should take a fancy to her—some older men had a taste for young women—but that he could offer her less than marriage and persist in doing so when she made it plain that she found his offer insulting, was amazing to her. "You know my views not at all," she said icily, "if you suppose that I would entertain an offer of carte blanche for any cause or with any assurances."

But Sir Nigel was proving impossible to snub. "I know," he said in an understanding way, "that you are gently bred and doubtless need time to think on the benefits of making such a step. If you *will* think on it, you will find that there are many, not the least of which is that you shall retain your freedom and have your future unhindered should you after all decide to marry at a later date."

"If anyone would have me," she said indignantly. "Please understand this, Nigel, for I do not intend to discuss this matter again. There is no consideration that would make me continue to think on your proposal. I do not need time. The answer is no, absolutely and with no chance of changing. If you wish any semblance of friendship to remain between us for my mother's sake, you will accept this and never mention this again. Certainly I shall not."

Willa had stated her rejection in such an unqualified way that it was incredible that this provoking man appeared in no way chagrined. He regarded her in merely a contemplative way and said, "I think it would be a mistake for you to be so certain. Haste is so often a source of regret."

His tone was insinuating and her anger and amazement were turning to disgust and a firm wish only to be rid of him. "Not in this matter," she said in a clipped way, and again gathered her reins to go after Leonora and Mr. Gordon, who were so far down the path ahead of them that they were nearly out of sight. But before she could leave him, Sir Nigel, who had one hand inside his coat, pulled this out, holding in his hand a small sheaf of papers that he held out to her.

Willa's impulse was to ignore him and go on, but the lure of wishing to know why he should proffer the papers to her was too great. She met his eyes for a brief, smoldering stare and then took the papers from him. At once she recognized them as bills, and her heart leapt into her throat even before she read to whom they were addressed or the amount they demanded. Her fears were justified. All were addressed to Sir Hammish Drake and a quick figuring of their combined total was staggering.

The control that Willa exercised over herself could prevent the shocked intake of her breath; Sir Nigel must know how she was affected. "Dear Lord, this is over ten thousand pound owing. But where have these come from? I am sure I have seen none of these before, certainly not the notes of hand. Why do you have them?"

"I own them," he said quietly.

Willa's brow creased. "What do you mean?"

Sir Nigel managed to look almost apologetic. "About a year before Sir Hammish died, he found himself in a bit of difficulty and asked if I could help him recoup his losses from an unfortunate investment. By good fortune, my own circumstances permitted me to pay for him the most pressing of his obligations, and as is the usual custom in such a case, I have since held the debts until payment could be expected." He paused and then added softly as if after thought, "Such as at the settlement of an estate."

"And why did you not present them when Papa died?" she asked suspiciously.

"I did not think the estate could bear such a sum. Can it?"

Willa smiled grimly. "I am sure you know it cannot." She resisted the temptation to go through the bills again to prove to herself that they were genuine, but that was clutching at straws. She handed the papers back to him and continued in a level tone, "Only the selling of the London house could realize such a sum."

"That would realize more than this paltry total."

"It may be paltry to you," she said with asperity, "but it is all the money in the world to me. I suppose there would be something left for us to live on, but it does not signify. We should certainly face the ruin that my mother so greatly fears. If you did not come forward when Papa died, why are you doing so now?"

He looked out upon the verdure that surrounded them. "Among *friends* arrangement may be made for payment to be put off indefinitely." He said no more; it was hardly necessary.

"I see," Willa said with a calm that surprised her. For the first time she felt the menace of the situation she was in, and was genuinely frightened. Her first and most natural wish was to respond to him with an unleashing of all the anger, rage, and hurt that was now ravaging her, but this was no time to be burning her bridges. The whole of her future, and even that of her mother and sister, could hang on this moment, and she could not be imprudent.

It was clear to her that if she accepted Sir Nigel's offer of carte blanche, she would be his "friend" and the debt would be allowed to continue; perhaps when he tired of her, he would dismiss it altogether as a parting gift. But if she stood her ground and her virtue, then the matter would revert to one of purely business and she and her family would face a financial ruin that no scheme of her making could possibly set to right.

"I don't know what to say to you," she said with perfect truth, trying not to sound as defeated as she felt. "I have no means of meeting my father's debt to you. You have been most generous to carry it so long," she added, wondering that she did not choke on the words. "I fear I must throw myself on your mercy and beg you to continue to do so for a bit longer."

"No doubt," he said smoothly, "you wish for a bit of time to think on your prospects. I can quite understand that."

Willa twisted her crop in her fingers, longing to strike him with it; instead, she managed a very credible smile. "Yes. As you have said, I was gently bred, and in spite of the superior education I received from my father, I am finding myself often unprepared to deal quickly with situations I have not encountered previously." Willa waited for him to press her less obliquely, but instead, he merely returned her smile in a way that she regarded as smug. But why should he not be smug? He was doubtless feeling very sure of his victory.

"It is not to be wondered at," he agreed. "But your father saw to your education because he had such a fine opinion of your intelligence and sense. I feel certain that you will not disappoint him, but will soon come to an amenable solution. I shall be leaving this afternoon for a visit to my sister, Lady Meering, in Kent for a few days—a sennight at best. When I return, I shall do myself the honor of calling upon you."

Willa did not misunderstand him. He would give her time to accept the fate he had in store for her, but not too much of it. She felt a sudden, almost overwhelming desire to dissolve into childish tears, but thought weeping an unprofitable exercise: she was a grown woman who had to face up to and deal with the problems that beset her. She raised her chin and met his impertinent gaze squarely.

"Your confidence in me is encouraging," she said with a sweetness so false that he must know her true feelings. "You may be sure I shall find a sensible answer to my dilemma."

He excused himself from going on with her and she was very glad of it. He did not even extend her the courtesy of riding with her until she caught up with Nora and Stephen, who had disappeared around a bend in the path; but she gave this no thought, and was merely thankful that he had left her. She urged her horse into a brisk canter and quickly found the young couple, who had stopped and were looking back along the path at her approach.

"We were just coming to find you," Leonora said with slight reproach. "I thought there must be some accident when we turned about and you had quite disappeared."

"We were lost in conversation and did not realize you were so far ahead. And," Willa added severely, "you need not think so poorly of my riding just because I am not the equal of you and Mr. Gordon. Even I must stay on a straight path in the park, though I am sure I should not care to take the lead of either of you on the hunting field."

They had all started back along the way that Willa had come and her quizzing was an attempt to keep either her sister or Mr. Gordon from asking how it was that they had become so separated. But Leonora could not be entirely deflected. She insisted on knowing why Sir Nigel no longer accompanied her sister.

"He had an appointment with some friends," Willa replied tersely, and again turned the subject.

Mr. Gordon escorted them to the edge of the park, and then, because he knew that he was not particularly welcome at Drake House by its mistress, he left them at the entrance to the park, looking after them for a very long time with a wistful expression.

3

Willa and Leonora, on returning home, went at once to their rooms to change; but as Willa did not come down for breakfast, Leonora, as soon as she had eaten, returned upstairs to find her sister. She found Willa, not in her bedchamber or sitting room, but on the ground floor in their papa's study, which was hardly entered anymore except by servants to keep the dust from overtaking the unused room.

Willa was sitting at her father's large oak desk at one end of the room near the tall windows. She was sitting in a dejected position, her arm across the pages of ledger, her head bent into her hands. For a moment, Leonora thought her sister was crying, but Willa so seldom wept. Leonora came quickly into the room, and when Willa raised her head at the sound of her approach, she was definitely dry-eyed, though her expression was glum enough to suggest tears were imminent.

Leonora perched on the edge of the desk. "What is amiss, Willa?" she asked with concern. "It is something to do with Sir Nigel, is it not? It was most peculiar that he did not return with you, and you have been abstracted, I think, since you were alone with him." She laughed a little as a thought occurred to her. "Never say that he has been making you an offer, too? I vow I am quite jealous, two in one week, Willa. I am quite cast in the shade."

"Sir Nigel did not ask me to be his wife," she was able to say without dissembling. "We were discussing quite another matter. I probably should not worry you with such a thing, but there are more debts of Papa's than we were aware of. Sir Nigel holds several bills that he paid for Papa, and notes of hand."

"Is it for very much?" Leonora asked very quietly.

Willa knew she had upset her sister and wished she had bitten her tongue. "Not really," she lied, "but it will require some juggling on my part, I fear, to see them paid." And that, Willa thought, was the greatest under-statement she had made in a twelvemonth.

"I need not have *all* my gowns made by Madame Céleste," Leonora offered, "and if it will help, you may sell the garnet set that Grandmama bequeathed to me, though I fear it may not fetch much."

Willa was touched by Leonora's concern and wish to help, but her economies would not have paid one of the vouchers she had seen that morning in the park. Willa assured her sister that these means would not be necessary and was surprised into dropping her pen by Leonora's next words.

"I don't suppose you could marry Sir Nigel?" Leonora said in all innocence. "He seems to be quite rich, and then we would not only not have to pay him, but would have settlements as well." She saw Willa's unexpected stricken look and said hastily, "But I am only roasting you, Willa. Of course you could not marry him; for one thing, he is quite old. I don't doubt that he is past the age of looking for a bride."

"Spoken with all the worldliness of eighteen summers," Willa said dryly. "Sir Nigel is far from his dotage or ready for pasture."

"Perhaps he just seems old to me," she conceded, "but I should not find his advances welcome."

This was a dangerous subject and Willa did not mean to pursue it. "And what of the advances of Stephen Gordon?" she asked in a quizzing way. "I can't believe he did not put his good forutne in finding himself unexpectedly alone with you this morning to good use."

Leonora blushed prettily. "I think he meant to ask me to marry him—you need not think you are the only one who receives offers—but I would not let him speak. I could not, you know, with Mama so objecting and our mourning not yet over."

Willa was silent for a moment. "I am not surprised; I have thought this his intention from the start. But you must have given him some hope, for he did not seem to me to be a rejected suitor when I joined you."

"I told him that I had promised Mama that I would not think of such things as marriage until I have been in the world more," Leonora said, avoiding Willa's gaze and playing with a crystal paperweight she had found on the desk.

"And did you make such a promise to Mama?"

Leonora nodded, and to her surprise, Willa did not berate her, but only said, "I suppose it is best, so that you will know your mind. *I* think you are very well suited to each other, but then, I do not have to live with the consequences if I am wrong."

"Very true," Leonora agreed without looking up. "I know you think me foolish to heed Mama on this head, but you know it is not just the things that she says to me. I should like to be a countess or a marchioness and live in great style. I know you do not care for such things, but we are not very alike, I think. You say that in marriage one must look to one's future harmony, but how happy should I be if I forever pined for a life I might have had?"

"What if you end pining for a love you might have had?" Willa asked slowly.

Leonora put down the paperweight and stood, taking an impatient turn about the room. "If you think Stephen so perfect, you should marry him yourself," she said a bit pettishly.

"I don't think he would have me," Willa said with a smile.

"Probably not," Leonora concurred. "If this were a perfect world, Stephen would be in love with you and Adam with me. Stephen is not perhaps bookish enough for you, but he likes a quiet life better than the racket of town; and Adam, with his fortune and title and good *ton*, would be a perfect match for me."

"Should he renew his offer," Willa said acerbically, "I shall be sure to tell him to apply to you."

"There will be a lot of languishing sighs when he does marry," Leonora said. "*You* may not think him a good match, but I can't think how many caps have been set for him. Cora Findlay told me her cousin Isobella Petrie would snap him up if he offered, but I don't think she is entirely respectable and Mama has told me men don't marry a woman who is careless of her reputation."

Willa caught at her breath. What would Leonora say if she knew her future might depend on her sister's joining the ranks of the demimonde? She had never heard of Isobella Petrie, but she was not so naïve as to suppose that there were no women in Adam's life. Yet, if this woman held a place in Adam's affections, it was not she with whom he contemplated marriage; that was the way of the world and of men. As she racked her brain for a solution to this newest dilemma, she had never seriously considered giving into Sir Nigel's proposal, and if in the bleakness of finding no easy answer, the base thought should occur to her, her younger sister's easy disdain of a woman who had lost her reputation must banish it at once.

"Perhaps there is some truth that I encourage Mr. Gordon for you because I like him myself, but I think my reasons for wishing you to favor him are better than Mama's urgings against him," Willa said, her manner a little constrained by the thoughts she could not share with Leonora. "I don't want to be as bad as Mama and try to push you in the way I would have you go, though. Just, please, be as sure as you can of your peace and happiness and let nothing else be a consideration."

Leonora came back to the desk and gave her sister a dimpled smile. "If I can manage it, I mean to have it all: love, companionship, fortune, and position," she said grandly.

Willa laughed. "I am sure I hope you may. But for most of us, I fear, the heart is a recalcitrant organ."

"You seem to have good command over your own," Leonora retorted with mock reproach. She meant nothing at all by the remark and Willa knew it, but she still felt somewhat disconcerted by it. In moments like this she wondered about her own cool approach toward marriage and if perhaps she felt as she did because she had no heart to easily give.

But the thought was just a reflection of her mood. When Leonora left a few minutes later, she returned to her task of making an informal accounting of their assets and which of these might be liquidated to meet her father's debt. Her task only confirmed what she already knew; to pay this debt would mean their coming down in the world and there was nothing to help it. They would not be out of the world entirely, of course, but Willa had previously witnessed families in financial ruin, and the drastic changes this made in their style of living inevitably resulted in their being cast into social oblivion. For herself it did not seem an unthinkable fate, but recalling Leonora's ingenuous confidence that she would like to be a figure in the fashionable world, she knew that for her it would probably mean the end of all choice. Willa might think her foolish to place importance on such things, but with all her heart she wished Leonora and her mother as well to have all in life that would bring them happiness.

She sighed, closed the ledger, and crumpled the papers full of figures that littered the desktop. Unbidden, she had in her mind a picture of Adam Revis, and it was accompanied by a feeling that was very like regret. She smiled a little to herself thinking that it was astonishing how real adversity served to put matters into perspective. If she had accepted Adam's offer on Monday, she could have snapped her fingers at Sir Nigel's offer today. But though the temptation to wish that she had been able to do so was strong, she knew in her heart that if Adam were to come into the room at this moment and repeat his offer, her answer must be the same. Marrying Adam for the wrong reasons was, to her mind, only a little better than becoming Sir Nigel's mistress to save the family fortunes.

Willa returned to her room, recalling, as she climbed the stairs, Adam's objections to her starting a school for select young ladies. She wondered what he would say if she told him of the choices she faced now, so much grimmer than a mere facing of social disapproval. With this thought she felt a keen desire to tell him everything, feeling intuitively that if there was a means of escape from her coil, his quick, clear-thinking mind would come up with it. But how could she reject him one day and run to him for his protection the next? He was too much a gentleman and a friend to withhold it, but she would feel sunk in shame to use him so. Her father had taught her to be self-reliant and had thought enough of her training to give his complicated affairs into her slender hands; somehow, she meant to prove equal to the task.

Willa quickly changed for the street and kept her appointment with Mr. Sledge, not, as she had originally intended, to discuss her plans for the school—for that was no longer to be thought of—but to go over with him her assessment of the value of their assets and to discover from him what he thought might reasonably be realized on them on short notice.

Mr. Sledge was most upset by this conversation and finally made a veiled threat to go to Lady Anne with information of her visit to persuade her to take him somewhat into his confidence. What Willa told him were half-truths, principally that she had discovered a further debt of her father's that she believed beyond the ability for the estate to absorb without the sale of capital. Try as he would, it was all the solicitor could pry from her and he was forced to be content with Willa's promise that, as soon as she could, she would make him aware of all the particulars.

Willa, too, came away from the interview less than satisfied. If anything, Mr. Sledge had taken a more pessimistic view of the money she would realize on the sale of the house and some other items than she herself had done, and she felt all but sunk in gloom during the short carriage ride back to Cavendish Square.

But Willa was not by nature a pessimist. It seemed to her that since the great blow of losing her beloved father, any number of lesser ones had continued to fall to her lot, but somehow the problems had always been met, and catlike, she remained on her feet. After all, this time she had a full sennight before the looming disaster was reality, and fate, that capricious lover, might just take pity on her and cast up a solution like driftwood on a shore.

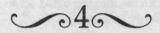

4

Adam Revis kept a fairly close watch on the main entrance
to the ballroom at Sefton House, but unlike Mr. Gordon,
who did the same, he managed to do it in such a way that
no one of the company in Lady Sefton's crowded apartments had the least notion of his vigilance. Mr. Gordon,
not so adept at dissimulation, seldom strayed from the
vicinity of the doorway and had already caused a comment
or two when he had visibly started at the entrance of some
fair young woman whom he mistook in his eagerness to be
Leonora Drake. Just turned thirty himself, but beyond the
pangs of first love, Adam sighed for the extremities of
youth and Eros and made his way to the side of Stephen
Gordon.

"I wouldn't expect her quite yet," he said softly and
without preamble. "Lady Anne enjoys an entrance and is
frequently among the last to arrive."

Stephen was acquainted with Lord Revis through their
mutual friendship with the Drake ladies, but they were
not on easy terms and he turned to the viscount to smile
uncertainly. "I-I find it cooler near the doorway," he said
with a somewhat lame attempt at dignity.

Adam gave him a brief, amiable nod. "As you say," he
agreed, and began to turn away, but Stephen, anxious

since this morning, when Leonora put him off, was in need of a confidant and Adam with his close relationship to the Drakes seemed made for the role.

"I suppose I am making a cake of myself," he said ruefully.

"Only a very small one," Adam replied with his slow smile. "Come with me into the cardroom to watch the play for a bit and give the gossips a rest."

Although Mr. Gordon obediently fell into step beside the viscount, as they reached the cardroom he could not resist a last glance over his shoulder toward the receiving line. He turned back to find Adam watching him with a bland expression, and colored a bit. "I want to persuade Nora to stand up with me for a country dance, if I can," he confided. "Her mourning has been so strict for much longer than is generally observed that there could be no objection to such a simple amusement."

"In general, no. But you will do yourself no good with Lady Anne if you suggest it. She is the highest of sticklers, you know."

"Don't I just know it," Mr. Gordon said flatly.

The cardroom was a large apartment annexing the ballroom and set up with numerous tables. A fair number of people, mostly gentlemen who did not care for dancing, were playing at whist, piquet, and even faro. Adam and Stephen walked casually among them, pausing now and again at a greeting from an acquaintance of one or the other, or to watch for a moment the play going forward. They declined an offer from the faro table to join the company there, and retraced their footsteps back to the ballroom.

"Perhaps," Adam suggested as they stood on the perimeter of the immense, lavishly decorated, and brightly lit room, "you should play up your connection to the illustrious Lord Byron. I have met him in Cavendish Square several times and I know that Lady Anne thinks highly of him. He is all that is fashionable, you know," he added at his blandest.

"I don't know that he will be for much longer," Stephen hinted, "and then I may be sorry to call him my cousin."

"Indeed?" said Adam, somewhat intrigued. "Keeping his name on everyone's lips for better or worse seems to be Lord Byron's forte, almost more so than his poetry, one might say."

"He enjoys being the center of a fuss," Mr. Gordon admitted. "Even the family is beginning to wonder, though, at his carelessness for his name. Mama hinted to me that she expects him to offer for Lord Milbanke's chit, Anabella, a good-enough match, but one almost wonders at Milbanke to entertain it. It might be a good thing, I think, if he does not. I don't know her well, but she seems to me a good-enough sort of girl; I know she is not at all in George's usual style. In fact, seldom have I seen a couple more ill-suited."

"You think suitability in marriage important?"

Mr. Gordon was surprised. "Of course. Isn't it?"

"Some people have rather high standards for it," Adam replied cryptically.

"Well, if it comes to that, it will be no difficulty for Nora and me. I think we are ideally suited in every way," Stephen said with a trace of defiance, "whatever Lady Anne may say and try to fill Leonora's head with. Miss Drake thinks so as well."

They were moving at a slow pace along the edge of the room back toward the principal entrance to the room. Adam stopped their progress. "You interest me, Mr. Gordon," he said. "I am not, ah, unacquainted with Miss Drake's views on the married state. Did she tell you why she thinks you and Leonora such a perfect matching?"

"Not in so many words," Mr. Gordon replied, a little

puzzled by the viscount's sudden attention. "But I am sure her views coincide with mine. We talked of it one day and she said she thought we would deal extremely well together and even suggested it might be no bad thing if I were to sweep Nora off her feet so that she didn't have time to think and weigh the advantages and disadvantages of all the notions she has in her head about making a grand match."

"I am astounded," said Adam, though he did not sound it. "Did she go to the length of suggesting a plan for this?"

Stephen Gordon looked uncomfortable and was wishing he had kept his tongue. "You must not think she was being serious; I am persuaded she would never truly wish me to do anything so improper."

"I never thought it," Adam assured him, "but I am curious what she said to you. Did she elaborate?"

"Well, she said something about hiring a coach and four and whisking Nora off to Gretna Green, but she was only jesting, of course."

"Of course."

A thought seemed to occur to Stephen and he added hopefully, "It would be improper, would it not?"

Whatever his own feelings, Adam had no intention of encouraging romantic folly. "It would indeed," he said with a half-smile, and allowed Mr. Gordon to be hailed away from him by one of that young man's friends. A particular friend of his own, Lord Hartley, came up to him about this time and remarked on Adam's uncommon pensiveness, but he could not tease Adam into revealing its cause.

The Drake party was not the last to arrive, but the ball was well under way and most young ladies present had the satisfaction of knowing their dance cards full by the time they arrived. Leonora, too young and eager to care for such things as a studied entrance, was inclined to be a bit peevish, but her mother pointed out, with an unmistakable hint of warning in her voice, that since there would be no dancing for her or Willa, it hardly mattered in any case.

Studied or unstudied, when they were announced they caused a definite stir among the assembled company. Polite society, ever in search of relief from perpetual ennui, found their return to the world interesting, so complete had been their withdrawal from the *ton*.

The picture of the three ladies framed by the entranceway was attractive enough to cause attention of itself. Lady Anne had insisted that though they had left off black, they should not wear colors beyond what was acceptable for half-mourning. She herself was magnificent in violet satin; three perfectly dyed and matched ostrich feathers waved grandly in her salt-and-pepper hair. Leonora, whose fairness did not lack color, was charming to behold in innocent white; and Willa, who knew well that pale colors made her look sallow, had chosen a simply cut gown of dark-gray silk, the severity of her style set off by cunning touches of black onyx at her ears and wrist and silver lace adorning her gown in unexpected places. In a room filled with soft pinks, blues, and greens worn by the younger girls and bold colors affected by the matrons, the Drake ladies must be striking in their difference.

Though he was half across the room, Stephen Gordon saw them enter at once; but remembering Adam's hint, he did not instantly go over to Leonora, but moved nonchalantly about the room for quite three full minutes before attaching himself to Leonora's side. As they moved among their friends and acquaintances receiving their welcome, Lady Anne's attention was at first distracted, but when she did notice the attendance of Mr. Gordon, her mouth set with annoyance. Only Willa, seeking to deflect her, called her attention to Lady Craven, who was waving to them, and thus saved Mr. Gordon from a heavy set-down.

But Lady Anne need not have been concerned that Mr. Gordon would monopolize her younger daughter. Before a quarter hour had passed, Mr. Gordon was routed. A court of young gallants surrounded Leonora, many of them known to her from her first Season, and Lady Anne had the satisfaction of overhearing her daughter described as a diamond of the first water.

Satisfied that Mr. Gordon would be only one of many admiring Leonora, Lady Anne immediately set about reestablishing herself as one of the more important matrons of the *ton* by renewing those contacts that her mourning had allowed to fade and by hinting that, as soon as the remaining weeks of relative seclusion were ended, there would be a return of the lavish and exclusive entertainments for which she was justly famed. The Prince Regent himself was among those who predicted that the cream of the *ton* would soon be panting for invitations to Drake House, and in one of his rare, willing-to-please humors, he played a gracious role in Lady Anne's social reinstatement.

The Seftons, though not especially known for their erudition, like most fashionable people, courted the intelligentsia of society, and Willa met there many old friends from the days of her father's Tuesday afternoon gatherings. Much whispered gossip in this set concerned George Gordon, Lord Byron. His mind and his talent were greatly admired, but his exhibitionism and disregard for the values of society were abhorred. Even his least scandalous affectations, such as his penchant for dining on potatoes and vinegar to keep his manly figure, or the suspicion that his angelic curls were artificially achieved, were endlessly discussed.

Because of his clubfoot, about which he was inordinately sensitive, Lord Byron did not dance, and he spent much of his time that evening beside Willa, who was similarly situated, though for a different reason. A number of young ladies who regarded Byron as quite the handsomest man in the realm, cast them black looks, of which Willa, who did not personally think of the poet in a romantic way, was unaware. Her disregard of their stares and the easy laughter she enjoyed with Lord Byron, who was in a particularly agreeable mood, started at least a few tongues wagging in their direction.

Mr. Gordon, who had scant interest in the entertainment now that he was reduced to the agony of watching Leonora made much of by half the bloods and fops in town (as he sardonically described Leonora'a admirers to Willa), decided to save Willa's reputation by making their *tête-à-tête* a threesome.

"Good God, has it come to this?" Bryon said with mock horror when Stephen piously stated the purpose of his mission. "Next it will be the reputation of my laundress at stake, and she a hundred at least and toothless."

"You've ever had a taste for the unique, George," Stephen remarked sweetly to his cousin.

The poet protested at this, but Willa laughed and said that she would take Stephen's words as a compliment to herself, to which the young lord could not demur. After a few more minutes' badinage with his two friends, Byron left them and Stephen took his place on the sofa beside Willa. They conversed in a desultory way, for each had heavy thoughts to distract, and when another friend of Willa's joined them a bit later, Stephen gradually dropped out of the conversation.

Willa did not at first notice this, but she had been attentive enough to note that Mr. Gordon's usual ready smile was a bit mechanical tonight, and she could well guess the cause, for as her observation increased, so did her realization that Leonora was so well entertained she seemed not even to notice his defection.

A parting in the company in front of them showed

Leonora seated on a similar sofa on an adjacent wall, the center of attention and clearly flirting with great delight with each of her admirers in turn.

Mr. Gordon was too proud a man to follow Leonora about the room with his eyes like a mooncalf, but Willa knew that he was constantly aware of her. Feeling for his pain, she suggested that they repair to one of the anterooms for refreshment so that he might not have to watch his beloved's perfidy. He may have been reluctant to leave the field entirely, but he rose with alacrity, his breeding prompting him to agree at once without the smallest hesitation.

"You must forgive Nora, Stephen," she said quietly as he handed her a glass of champagne punch. The sets for the next dance were forming and the room held only another couple who were far enough from them not to overhear what they might say. "This night is almost as exciting to Leonora as was her first presentation. It is nice to know that one is not forgotten."

He understood her but shook his head sadly. "What are my claims to those of Lord Seton or the Marquess of Perth? It is not unexpected. I know that Leonora enjoys attention. It isn't that which I mind, but that she seems to find me *de trop* tonight."

"I am sure it is no such thing," Willa said, and then fell silent for a few minutes. "I think," she continued, "that Nora just needs to try her wings for a bit. I fear that Papa's death, coming when it did, just as she was making her bow to the world, clipped them untimely."

"And as soon as she learns to soar, she will be content to roost in my nest?" He laughed in a self-disparaging way. "You need not spoon-feed me, Willa; I know what competition I face. Seton and Perth for two; there will be others, I think."

Willa could not honestly gainsay this or give Stephen

the comfort he craved. But Leonora was not a fool and she had observed as well as Willa how unhappy one could be married to the wrong person. In her heart, Willa believed that Leonora, when she made her choice, would do so as sensibly as she would herself. She said this much to the unhappy young man beside her.

But Mr. Gordon did not appear to be particularly buoyed by her words. "I hope you may be right," he said, "but with Lady Anne so set against me and the persistence of suitors as illustrious as Seton and Perth, *I* would not give odds for my success."

The dance ended and the room began to fill with the participants come to refresh themselves before the next set formed. Stephen and Willa drifted back into the ballroom, and after returning Willa to a quiet corner of the room as she requested, he excused himself to have another try at establishing his position at Leonora's court.

Though Willa had not looked for Adam conspicuously since her arrival and had refrained from asking anyone if he was present, she frequently scanned the company as unobtrusively as possible for his tall figure. He had told her that he would attend the ball and she was aware of an unexpected sense of disappointment.

The company at most parties did not always remain constant; it was common for many guests to attend more than one event a night, dividing their time between them. Since her party had arrived late, it was possible that Adam had already come and gone. For some reason she found the thought dispiriting, and wondered that she should.

Unable to dance, an activity she enjoyed, and finding the conversation, even with the more erudite of the company, insipid tonight, Willa was becoming quickly bored; she wished, not for the first time at such a social event, that she had stood up to her mother and insisted on remaining home, where she might have been better occupied with a book or catching up on her correspondence.

When the musicians struck the first chord of a waltz, one of two to be played that night, the acquaintance who had stopped to chat with her, being fortunate enough to be approved and have a partner for the dance, left her, and for the first time that evening, she was alone. The waltz was a dance still considered shocking by some for the headiness of its movement and the close embrace of the partners. Not everyone was permitted to dance it without courting social disaster, and the young, unmarried women who had not the approval of the leaders of society to do so, formed small disconsolate-looking groups in the corners of the room, laughing too loudly and tossing their curls in apparent indifference as they watched their favorite swains lead rivals into the breathless pace of the dance.

Willa, though she loved to waltz, did not especially envy the participants and lost herself to the pleasure of the music. Enrapt, she did not notice Adam's approach until he sat beside her on the sofa. She turned her head and her expression of polite inquiry unconsciously turned to one of plainly shown pleasure as she beheld him. He responded to this welcome with a swift smile, and seeing him look at her so, Willa felt an involuntary response that had little to do with friendship.

Turning away from him again, she said a bit coolly to distance her feelings, "I had begun to think I would not see you tonight, my lord."

" 'My lord?' Have I done something to offend you into formality? Do you know that for a moment I thought you were quite glad to see me. Was I wrong?" He paused and then added before she could reply, "Dear me, I hope that asking you to marry me hasn't frightened you into wishing me at arm's length. I shall keep my promise not to plague you about it, you know."

"Of course it has not," Willa replied with a little constraint, for he put her in mind that the last time they had spoken she had rejected him. "I am glad to see you, but . . ."

"You feel a bit awkward with me?" he said helpfully. "My dear girl, if you do not hold it against me for asking, I certainly shall not hold it against you for refusing. I assure you, I wear my chagrin in private. What would truly upset me would be if our friendship were affected."

"It isn't, Adam," she said, making herself look up at him with a smile. "I don't know why I am behaving so missish; it is not really like me."

"So I know." A small silence fell between them and after a bit he said carefully, "I can't help feeling that there is something amiss. I hope you think me friend enough to help you in any difficulty."

Willa knew him to be a man of keen perception, but had not thought herself so transparent to be so easily read. The words her pride would have her speak—that all was well—formed on her lips, but sudden, unaccustomed tears stung at her eyes. Feeling curiously detached, she told him in a flat voice that she had discovered new debts that must be paid at once, even to the point of selling the house. He was not so easily put off as Mr. Sledge and managed to garner the information from her that the holder of these debts was Sir Nigel Allerton. But she had enough of her wits about her not to tell him that Sir Nigel had made her an offer of his own, or was using her father's notes as a means to try to force her to compliance.

As she spoke, his lids, always heavy, drooped even more and his expression became so shuttered that she could not guess what was in his mind. She expected him to question the amount she mentioned or the drastic means she meant to employ to realize the sum, but instead he asked, "Why has Allerton brought these to you now? They should have been presented with the rest of Sir Hammish's debts when the estate was settled."

Willa was a little nonplussed by this. "He—he did not wish for us to be overwhelmed in our first grief," she said with hasty invention.

"But you are not more able to pay him now than then."

"No."

"Then, what was the point of his concern?" he said with a hint of sardonicism. "I gather he wishes for speedy payment, and I don't understand that either. Perhaps I mistake that he is a particular friend of Lady Anne."

"He is," she admitted, wishing that she had had the sense never to mention the matter to him at all. "Perhaps he has need of the money himself. I did not inquire; it was enough to know that the debt exists and must be paid. In fact, it hardly matters; we shan't have a sum that vast to pay him next month or next year. I don't think he can be blamed."

"Don't you?" said Adam with curiosity. "No doubt I am overnice in my notions, but I cannot think well of him for it. You may not like this, but I shall offer anyway. Will you let me help you in this?"

Willa, who had been looking at the dancers to avoid meeting his direct gaze, glanced at him quickly. "If you can think of some means of finding the money from the estate, I should be grateful for your advice, but," she added repressively, "if it is a loan that you have in mind, thank you but I would not take it."

"I thought you would say that," he said, not at all offended. "Suppose I bought the vouchers from Allerton and made you a gift of them on your next birthday; suppose you will tell me it is too grand a gift."

Willa laughed slightly. "You know me too well, Adam. And if you are thinking to do it behind my back, it will avail nothing, for I shall pay you, and as quickly as I would Sir Nigel."

Adam might have been adept at concealing his thoughts, but he could not repress an exasperated sigh. "You say that you will let me help you, but then you make it impossible," he complained. He was at times accused of being a proud man, but he felt that his pride was well matched by her own. He applauded her as a woman of spirit, but he took her rejection of his person in better part than he did his purse. But he could be as determined as she, and he meant to assume this untimely burden for her.

He was almost tempted to renew his offer of marriage, but he knew he would be rejected again and he would upset her as well. His offer for her had not been impulsive except in its timing, and even as he was speaking, he knew that he was precipitate. This time his judgment would reign over his emotions; he had no intention of making a career of making her unwanted offers.

One quality that most of Adam's friends admired in him was his resourcefulness. When forced to think on his feet, his mind was razor-sharp. A sudden thought, a quick memory flashed into his fertile brain, the seed planted by his conversation with Stephen Gordon. It was an outrageous thought; he wondered if he dared suggest it to her. But Adam was also a successful gamester, knowing just when to be daring and when to hedge his bets. His instinct, which so seldom failed him, told him it was time to be bold.

He was silent for so long after his remark that Willa began to feel concern. "Oh, dear, I have offended you, haven't I? I am *most* grateful for your wish to help me—"

He cut her short with a motion of his hand. "I understand you, I don't like the feeling of owing a friend any more than you do," he said briskly, and then smiling in his languid way, he let his voice drift into a fashionable drawl. "You do consider me your friend, don't you, Willa?"

"You know I do," Willa replied, bemused.

"Then will you trust me and consider another proposition I have to offer?"

Willa was instantly wary. The last thing she wished was that he renew an offer of marriage for convenience. "You need offer me nothing, Adam," she said, gently dampening. "Listening to my troubles has been more than enough. I could not confide this in Nora or Mama, for they are touched as nearly as I by this."

"That is all very well, but you need something a bit more practical than a shoulder to cry on at the moment," he pointed out. "Do you think I mean to ask you to marry me again?" he said shrewdly, raising a faint guilty tint in her cheeks. "I have quite something else in mind."

Reassured that he did not mean to renew his suit, Willa was impatient to hear him, but the waltz had ended and the participants were returning to the perimeters of the room to rest or find their next partners, and their privacy would soon end.

"Not here," he insisted, and led her out into the main hall and down a short corridor. They passed through the first open door into a small, dimly lit room.

The door was, of course, left open, but Willa felt conscious of their intimacy and blamed her inability to stop harking back to his proposal of Monday. She told herself it was nonsense, but she deliberately sat in one of two chairs in a conversational setting, conspicuously avoiding the sofa.

If Adam sensed her unease, he made no comment, but she thought she saw a faint mocking light play in his eye as he himself sat across from her on the sofa. He regarded her for a long moment and then said in his lazy, pleasant voice, "Run away with me to Scotland."

Willa was startled into a short laugh. "Adam! Are you castaway?"

He placed his right hand over his heart. "No more than two glasses of champagne tonight, upon my honor."

"Then you are roasting me," she said darkly, "which is really too bad of you, Adam, when I am in such difficulties. I thought you had hit upon something to help me."

"I have," he persisted. "Come with me to Scotland. We need remain only a sennight or even less, and when we return, I shall pay off Allerton and put a similar sum into the funds in your name."

Dark suspicion filled Willa and made her feel cold inside. "You aren't drunk, but I wish you were," she said icily.

Adam was not abashed; he laughed. "Dear Lord, Willa, you know me better than this. I am not offering to give you a slip on the shoulder."

The cant phrase was unfamiliar to her, but she understood it to be that he was not attempting to offer her carte blanche as Sir Nigel had done. "Then, what are you offering me?"

Leaning one arm on the sofa, he cupped his head in his hand and recounted his hastily concocted scheme. "I have an aunt who lives in Scotland, not far from the infamous Gretna, in fact. She is my mother's only sibling, and as Mama had married so well and has small need of it, she inherited most of my grandfather's fortune, to which I am now sole heir. Several days ago, I had a letter from her informing me that if I did not repent my wicked ways and the sins of my youth and settle down with a comfortable wife, she would leave the whole away from me.

"It is not a question of needing the inheritance," he continued, his heavy eyes quietly watchful for her reaction, "but her threat is to leave it out of the family altogether to a naturalist set she has gotten involved with of late bacause they have convinced her that the diet they prescribe soothes her gout. It is relief she is seeking, not discipleship, and they would inherit more to spite me than because Aunt Maria wishes them to have the means to spread their ideology."

"I think, my lord," Willa said with mock indignation, "that this puts your flattering offer to me in quite a different light. I thought you had been devastated by my charms."

"Oh, but I am," he said, smiling. "Yet it would have been a very good thing, don't you think," he added outrageously, "if we could have helped each other out of our difficulty, if you had been willing to have me."

"A true marriage of convenience," Willa said, laughing, but though she did not at all wish for him to be languishing for her, she could not help being piqued by his practicality in offering for her. "But just because I may now acquit you of misguided nobility, it does not make me wish to be married any more than I did before."

"I told you I was not offering you that again," he said. "I only want you to come with me to Canonbie and pretend to be my wife. My aunt is a near recluse and does not go into society at all. She is quite old, you see, my mother's elder by a full ten years, and unwell. It is very unlikely that the imposture would ever be detected and it need be known to very few."

Willa did not know what to think. "I fear you are not drunk, but mad. I could not do such a thing, Adam! How can you suggest it?"

"Why not? You won't be compromised, I give you my word on it, and you will be earning the money, not making a loan or taking charity. Are you worried about the improprieties? They shall be seen to, I promise you, and you need have no fear I shall think your accepting means more than it does."

He had covered her every objection, but she could not

be convinced. "It's impossible, and more than that, dishonest."

"My Aunt Maria is a very managing woman," he said. "One of the reasons we need not fear exposure is that she has quarreled with most of her relatives over the years, including my sister. I am the last one of my mother's family with whom she corresponds." He sighed. "I am sorry if this will make you think poorly of me, but I have no compunction at all over wishing to trick her. She could leave Grandfather's money to my sister or some cousin with my blessing. It is that she seeks to control me by this, for she knows that I would dislike her threat. She would use me, Willa; I have hit upon the means of staying her scheme."

Though she thought to refuse him absolutely, in the back of her mind her thoughts ran riot over how it could be accomplished in a way that would not so openly court scandal. "You could not possibly know that I would not be compromised. I might simply trade one sort of ruin for another."

The faint smile that lifted the corners of his mouth might have held a hint of triumph. By her words he knew she was not going to reject him again out of hand. "I think you know I would not let that happen," he said quietly.

Willa understood him, but did not respond.

"Come," he said almost plaintively. "Is it so unbearable a fate to contemplate?"

"Of course not," she said, a little ashamed of her hesitation, "but if I do not wish to be married for convenience, neither do I wish it simply to avoid a scandal."

"You concern yourself overmuch, Willa," he assured her. "My aunt has no wish to puff off my marriage, only to know that it has been accomplished according to her will."

Willa seemed to think on this and said after a moment,

"You have an answer for everything, don't you? Have you been planning this all along?"

"Not at all," he said truthfully. "It simply occurred to me tonight that since you were desperate but would not take help in a conventional form, we might find a means of serving each other."

Willa's laugh was a little uncertain; she still did not know her mind. "I think you must be the most honest man I know. Another would have couched it in more flattering terms."

"Another man would probably not have proposed it at all, unless he had something quite different in mind," he said with disarming frankness. "I have shocked you a little, I think. It *is* a solution, you know, and your choices don't seem to be many. Surely it is better than selling up everything and living as shabby genteels in some dingy little box in Kensington."

Willa regarded him for a long moment, her confusion obvious. "I think my character must not be the bastion of virtue I thought it, for you tempt me greatly."

"Your virtue won't come into it, my dear Willa. Follow your instincts," he advised her in his soft drawl. "You won't regret it, I think."

Willa wished she might say that her instincts told her to run from him and his mad scheme, but they did not. "What of Mama? I could not leave for what would surely be a fortnight without saying where I was to go, and I promise you that Mama will be even harder than me to convince to such a scheme. She has a very nice sense of propriety, you know, and she will probably be shocked into forbidding you the house if I tell her."

"Does she know of this debt? No? Then tell her and tell her what I have proposed to you and the reassurances I have made to you. Lady Anne is a practical woman; I think she will listen."

"She might listen, but she would never agree," Willa said pessimistically.

"You won't know that until you ask her."

Willa's expression was doubtful. "There is no point in that yet, when I do not even know if I could go along with such a thing." She rose and, smiling, said, "If I do not soon rejoin the company, I shall not have to worry about my reputation, it will be in tatters."

He stood with her. "But will you think on it, Willa?"

Taking in her breath and letting it out again quickly, Willa nodded, for she knew she could not dismiss this as she might wish to. A moment later she left him, entering the hall carefully, already fearful of the prying eyes of gossips.

Adam was not displeased with their interview or the progress of their dealings. Finding herself in distress, she had come at once to him; he found this vastly encouraging. When this outrageous plan had come into his mind, he had more than half-expected her to reject it out of hand; she had not. His hopes were really very high.

He had detailed his idea for her rescue exactly as he had thought it up, but now, as he slowly made his way back to the ballroom, another idea, in its way even more outrageous, struck him with much force. Once again his gamester's instincts were to the fore. He wasted only another moment or two in plotting and then at once sought out Lady Anne Drake.

5

Willa had already confided a portion of her dilemma to Leonora, so it was a simple step to take her further in her confidence and admit that the debt was after all a great one and that Adam Revis had concocted a shocking plan to overcome it. Leonora was not unconscious of the burden that was on her older sister, and she tried not to show her upset at the discovery that they were soon to be all to pieces, but Willa was able to read her feelings with fair accuracy. When she told her of Adam's plan, she agreed it was improper and that of course Willa must do as she saw best; yet Willa began to feel that her own objections were trite when compared to the good she might do for Leonora and her mother. When Willa asked her plainly if she thought that she should discuss the matter with her mother, Leonora said yes with such alacrity that Willa allowed her mind to be made up for her. They agreed between them that it might be best not to mention Sir Nigel's name, as it would only upset Lady Anne the more.

Lady Anne displayed a natural horror that such a dismal fate might await her, especially now when she had quite convinced herself that their financial difficulties were all but behind them.

"Perhaps it is a hoax," Lady Anne suggested without

conviction. "I am not at all sure that I trust Mr. Sledge, such an obsequious little man. I should not be at all surprised if he were in league with some Captain Sharp for a commission."

"I would certainly be surprised," Willa replied. "Mr. Sledge would not take so dim a view of my wits or suppose my nature to be so trusting. The debts are genuine, Mama."

They were in their mother's sitting room: Willa, feeling restless, did not sit but stood in front of one of the windows, moving about a bit from time to time; Lady Anne, as was her usual custom, reclined in a chaise longue; and Leonora, looking glummer by the minute, sat uneasily on the edge of a straight-backed chair. Willa, glancing toward her, saw that her cheeks were wet with silent tears. "I'm so sorry, Nora. I know it seems dreadful just now."

"It *is* dreadful," Leonora said on a sob. "Oh, I did not mean to say so to you, but it is. Lord Seton asked last night if he might call upon me this morning and he was all attention last night. What will he think when he finds that we are to be paupers living in some desperate little rooming house or some such thing?"

"On some back street in Kensington," said Lady Anne, pronouncing the last word like an epithet. "We *are* ruined. I knew just how it would be; Sir Hammish was the most unfeeling of men. You must do something, Willa."

Willa was a little struck by her mother's describing their fate in terms so similar to those that Adam used. "We have not come to that yet, Mama," Willa said gently, and completed her story, telling her of Adam's proposal of the previous night. Willa expected her to be insulted and to wonder why he offered such a scheme when he might have offered her marriage in an honorable way; she was very much loathe to tell her mother of Adam's original offer and her refusal of it. Lady Anne might well fall into a fit of the vapors to discover that her daughter had whistled such a suitor down the rainpipe.

But Lady Anne listened with attention and Willa saw no sign of indignation clouding her brow. When Willa had done, her response was most astonishing to her daughers. "Thank goodness for our friends," she said with undisguised relief.

Leonora was dabbing at her eyes with a delicate square of lace, but she stopped and said, "Mama, do you mean that you *wish* Willa to go to Scotland with Lord Revis? You have forbidden me to drive out as far as Richmond in the company of a gentleman unless we are of a large party."

"It is hardly the same thing," Lady Anne said acerbically. "There is nothing to be gained in flouting propriety in the general way, but this is quite another matter. Nor is your sister a green girl as you are."

Wondering if perhaps her mother had not quite understood her and the risk to her reputation, Willa quickly reiterated the outline of Adam's plan, deliberately emphasizing that she would not only have to travel the length of the country in Adam's company, but she would also have to pretend to be his wife once they reached Scotland. She had thought that, carefully choosing her words, she might be able to convince her mother to allow her to go, but she never expected that Lady Anne would wish her to do so without demur.

Yet that was the case. "It is a mad scheme," she agreed, "but what else is to be done? Do you wish to spend the rest of your life in penury, the object of pity and charity to your friends? Assuming we shall still have any. Poverty and social oblivion are bedfellows."

"Will you do it, Willa?" Leonora asked, not quite able to keep the hopefulness out of her voice. "I own I thought it unseemly at first, but if Mama cannot object . . . it would be so nice to have all our bills paid and a sum in the funds as well so that we do not have to pinch our pennies so much." If she could not help sounding wistful, she added, in loyalty to her sister, "Of course, if you feel you could not, Mama and I shall understand."

"You may speak for yourself, miss," declared Lady Anne, sitting up abruptly. "It is a piece of nonsense to be missish over a fortnight's work when the situation is desperate. Were matters otherwise with us," she conceded, "it would not do to think of it, of course."

Willa, who was making a restless turn about the room, stopped before her mother's couch and said, "It is an improper and even dangerous thing to do, but I fear you are right. In other circumstances the answer must be no, but as they are, it *must* be thought of. My biggest concern is maintaining discretion. What good would it be to be saved from financial ruin if in doing so I heaped another kind of disgrace upon us?"

"We must take great care that you do not," Lady Anne said firmly. She indicated for Willa to sit beside her on the sofa. "I have thought on it and I think I know what we must do."

"Thought on it?" Willa said, surprised. "But, Mama, I have only just told you."

"We have been discussing it this half-hour. Do you suppose that you and your father were the only members of this family capable of quick, clear thinking?" she said haughtily. "In matters of propriety and *ton*, I fancy I could have taught Sir Hammish a thing or two, and you as well, miss."

"Yes, Mama," Willa said with unusual meekness, and prepared to listen attentively to her mother's plan.

"At first I thought that perhaps I might accompany you, but then I realized that if anything did go awry, it would look as if I had countenanced an indelicate situation; that would do neither of us any good. Leonora will go with you," she said decidedly. "We shall say that you are visiting friends in Yorkshire; it is just the thing! Adam, as a friend of the family, will escort the carriage—riding beside it, of course—for he has business in the area and must travel there in any case. It would be best, of course, if we need not involve Nora, but you must have proper chaperonage and there is no one whom we would dare to take into our confidence in this matter."

Both daughters were astonished at this speech, though for different reasons. "Oh, Mama," Leonora said on a near wail, "I have only just gone into the world again. Lord Seton is calling, and likely Lord Perth as well, and I have had all manner of invitations for drives and rides in the park and—"

"Are you forgetting, Nora," said her mother severely, "that if we do not make it possible for Willa to go, there will be no invitations at all? In any case, I hope you were not so hoydenish that you accepted any invitations without my sanction. We are not out of mourning for your papa until the end of next month."

Acknowledging the truth of this and begging pardon, Leonora subsided unhappily, and Willa spoke out, saying carefully, "But who shall we say we are visiting? Most of our friends in Yorkshire come to town for the Season and would easily give us the lie."

"There is no need to elaborate," Lady Anne informed her. "In the first place, a detail of inquiry is an impertinence that can be dealt with, and in the second, if we were pressed to it, it would be easy enough to invent an elderly cousin or something of that nature. I don't really expect it will be necessary. We will simply return to our retirement until the end of May, which will not be wondered at; your absence may scarcely be noticed."

"But Lord Seton is calling this morning," said Leonora,

her mind focusing on the thing most important to her, "and I told Lord Perth and Mr. Hollaran that I should surely see them at Mrs. Christie's on the eighteenth, for you had said we should go to her party. They will surely note *my* absence."

"And there is Mr. Gordon, who is bound to call as well," Willa reminded her quietly.

But in the rush of her newfound popularity, Leonora had all but forgotten her most faithful admirer. "Yes, him, too," she said in a dismissive way. "They will have to be told something, Mama."

"You may leave all safely to me, my dear," Lady Anne assured her, rising. The door into the hall was ajar and the bell was heard from below. "Doubtless that is Seton now. You need not disturb yourself, Nora," she said to her. "I shall see Lord Seton myself, for it is best if we take matters in hand at once. Willa, write out a note for Lord Revis and ask him to call on you as soon as may be for your answer."

At that moment a footman scratched on the door to announce the arrival of the earl, and when Lady Anne had left them, Willa remained seated on the sofa regarding her sister, who was staring in a disconsolate way at the handkerchief she had balled in her hands.

"I am sorry, Nora," Willa said very gently. "More than anything I wanted you to have this Season exactly as you would wish it. But take heart, it will only be for a fortnight, and as Mama says, then we may be comfortable again. If all goes well," she could not forbear adding.

"I really don't mind accompanying you," Leonora said with an attempted smile. "I have never been to Scotland, you know, and it is such a pretty time of year to travel, I expect I shall enjoy it. It is only that I wish it were not quite now that we had to go," she added, her countenance darkening again. "I daresay that by the time I return, Lord

Seton and all the other gentlemen who were so kind to me last night will have forgotten all about me."

"In a fortnight?" Willa said with a laugh. "You don't rate your charms very high, do you, goose?"

"There are so many girls just coming out this year who are so much prettier than I," Leonora said with innate modesty. "If I am not there to make them notice me, I am sure I do not see why they should."

"Any man whose memory is that poor or whose affections are that fickle," Willa said caustically, "strikes me as an unlikely candidate for *your* affections. Mr. Gordon would not use you so."

Leonora gave a watery giggle. "Oh, Willa! I wish *you* would marry Stephen and be done with it."

Willa laughed with her, aware that she probably did Mr. Gordon no favor by pushing him on Leonora. Commenting that she might as well go to her room and fetch her needlework if this was to be another dully spent day, Leonora left, and Willa got up and began to pace about the room again.

She had the feeling of being on a carousel, whirling about and uncertain of where she would end up. All the objections she had imagined and had thought she would have to counter had never materialized. Instead of being glad, she felt a little deflated. The execution of Adam's proposal, which had seemed at first to her so outrageous and absurd, was going to go forward with no more regard to its consequences than if it were a commonplace.

Perversely, the total lack of opposition she found to it from her mother and sister made her wishful of backing away from it, at the very least for time to give it more thought. But there really was no time for this luxury, and she knew it. In little more than a week, she would have to give Sir Nigel his answer, and by that time she wanted with all her heart to be able to snap her fingers at him.

There was only one way she could do that. It was true that if she went to Scotland, she would still be there when Sir Nigel returned, but it gave her no concern that he would be forced to cool his heels for another sennight. She even wondered if it might be possible to arrange with Adam to have him paid discreetly through Mr. Sledge while she was away; it would be treating Sir Nigel like a tradesman, but she felt he deserved the insult; in fact, the prospect of it gave her a decided satisfaction. When next she met Sir Nigel (as surely she must), she would accord him common civility for her mother's sake and to show her breeding, but she doubted that after such treatment even he would ever dare to broach the subject of his proposal and attempted coercion again.

Willa spent the remainder of the morning drafting the brief letter that she sent to Adam. As she wrote the discreetly worded message in a number of different ways, the unease of her mind grew. She chided herself for a prude, but somehow she did not think that it was that that was the sticking point for her.

Eventually she found the right words to say to him, accepting but not eager, cooperative but not compliant. She called for a footman to deliver the note by hand and bid him take it at once, for she did not trust herself not to tear up even this last effort in hopes of finding a clearer word or better turn of phrase.

It utterly astonished her how rapidly matters were in hand, once it had begun. Adam called at once, and after an hour spent with her and her mother working out all the details and attempting to foresee every possibility of risk to Willa's reputation and finding measures to counter these, that very Tuesday was settled upon for the start of their journey.

Leonora, once all the details were settled, accepted her

return to retirement with good grace. When Willa confessed doubts to her about the felicity of the plan, it was
she who buoyed her elder sister's spirits with an optimistic
practical approach to all, and on the whole she seemed to
be regarding it as an adventure.

On Tuesday morning, a scant four days after the ball
when she had confided in Adam, his well-sprung, crested
traveling chaise and a more serviceable vehicle for the
servants and baggage drew up before the house in Cavendish Square.

Though Adam had assured them that his aunt lived
quietly and did not entertain, Lady Anne had insisted that
her daughters be prepared and adequately outfitted for any
eventuality, with the result that the entrance hall was
virtually jammed with their baggage for a mere fortnight's
journey.

"And half of that time will be spent on the road," Willa
said with a resigned sigh and an apologetic smile for Adam.
He nobly refrained from commenting on the clutter, but
his eyes widened perceptibly at the sight of one trunk,
several portmanteaus, a large dressing case, and two
bandboxes.

"At least we shall impress my aunt with the consequence of my bride," he said with the lift of one brow.

Willa cast a nervous glance about the room for a footman or maid who might have overheard the remark, but
they were momentarily alone.

He saw her nervousness and smiled in his lazy way. "I
knew we were alone. I have promised you I won't compromise you, and you have nothing to fear of me, you know."

"Can you really have lived your whole life in houses
with servants and not know that the walls have ears?" she
said a little impatiently. "The things you can't shout in the
street are best left unsaid."

"Do you think so?" he asked, looking much struck. "How confining, and how dull!"

But as the Drake butler, Biddle, entered with a footman in his wake, he smoothly turned the conversation to commonplaces like the weather he expected they would encounter as they traveled north during such an unsettled season.

"You will see it is exactly as I have said," interrupted Lady Anne as she came into the hall from a side corridor, "one or two light muslins apiece will not come amiss should the weather turn unseasonably warm, as it is wont to do during the spring. Did you remember to pack your vinaigrette, Willa? I know you think you will not need it, but what if there is a mishap to the carriage? No lady is ever wise to travel without it."

Willa was spared having to answer this by the arrival of her sister from upstairs; she was dressed superbly in a russet-hued carriage dress and matching bonnet that seemed more appropriate for the park than a long journey. Nor was it in keeping with Lady Anne's wish for them to remain at least in half-mourning, but she looked so fetching that not even her mama demurred, and Willa, feeling quite dowdy in an old brown habit, supposed that Leonora had dressed so to keep up her spirits. Willa determined that she would not allow Leonora to be sorry for accompanying her.

After several more minutes spent in last-minute checks to be sure that nothing was forgotten (if that were possible) and a number of admonitions from Lady Anne for their safety and comfort on the road, Willa, Leonora, and the abigail they shared, Betsy, were at last assisted into the chaise. Adam rode beside them on a spirited chestnut and meant to do so at least for as long as the weather held fine.

This proved to be the case until their third night on the road. The carriages, designed to be light and pulled each by four horses, with spare teams from his lordship's own stables sent on ahead for several stages, made most excellent time, almost equal to the fast-traveling mail coach. Though Adam admitted that he was being optimistic, he still maintained, as they sat in a private parlor at the Brown Doe near Hawes, that it was entirely possible that they reach their destination before night fell the following day and thus avoid another night on the road.

"And," he added as large raindrops began to spatter against the panes of the room's sole window, "even if I am mistaken and we are forced to stop before reaching the border, it is still a considerable improvement over the five nights on the road I recall being necessary when I was a boy and chaises were not so well sprung."

Willa sat with an unladylike slouch in a wing chair. Despite the comfort of the carriage, traveling nearly from sunup to sundown for three days straight was wearing to say the least. "Your father probably hadn't the foresight to send his own horses ahead for half the journey," she said with a note of sarcasm. "I should think you will need the inheritance from your aunt by the time we return to town."

"Are you complaining?" asked Leonora, incredulous. "I, for one, could not be happier that Adam has been so thoughtful. Traveling is such a tedious thing to do."

"Commenting, not complaining." Willa regarded her sister, who was absently following the pattern of selected raindrops as they hit the panes. "I still wish you did not have to be a part of this deception," she said abruptly.

"There was no choice," Leonora said fatalistically. "And it will be worth it in the end."

"The disaster will be averted, certainly," Willa said dampeningly, "but you must not suppose that our lives will change overmuch. We shall still have to be mindful of our income. Adam has been most generous, but I think I shall still look into the notion of beginning a school."

"I am completely optimistic," Leonora said, coming away from the window to sit at the table. She rested her chin in her hands and cast a brief, knowing glance toward Adam.

Willa, observing this, thought that Adam frowned a little at Leonora, but the expression was so fleeting that she could not be certain that an actual exchange had taken place.

They had been shown at once into the private parlor while their bedchambers were made ready, and considerable time had passed since without any servant arriving to take them to their rooms or discover their needs.

Getting up from his chair near the fire, Adam said, "I am not at all optimistic about the service we shall receive at this inn. I think perhaps it is time for me to make the innkeeper aware of my consequence." He paused in the threshold of the door into the taproom. "It is quite the best thing about having consequence, you know."

"I quite agree," said Leonora, her eyes dancing. "Throw your title about a bit; that should answer."

"But of course," he agreed. "Viscounts may be obliged to bow and scrape to earls, marquesses, and dukes, but we know well what is due to us from barons on down the social scale to innkeepers." Putting a rather supercilious expression into place on his handsome features, he went out into the common room, closing the door behind him.

"I hope this may be our last night on the road," Willa said with feeling. "I begin to understand why Mama and Papa always insisted on traveling in easy stages. A leisurely, broken journey is certainly less tiring."

Leonora agreed, and shortly after Adam returned to them, assuring them that he had successfully chivied the landlord and his staff, a chambermaid arrived to escort them to their apartments to refresh themselves for dinner.

Dinner, when finally procured, was excellent and well served, and the bedchambers allotted to them met with the full approval of each, being roomier and more comfortable than most to be found on the road. Sleep came easy with so much to induce it, but Willa woke early, even before Leonora, who was a habitually early riser. She was bathed and dressed before Leonora was even out of bed and she went down stairs at once.

Adam was already down, which did not surprise her, but he was in the coffee room speaking with a liveried young man and a young woman, which did. Willa recognized the pair at once, for they were her mother's own servants. As soon as he perceived her, the footman started toward her and with a brief bow proffered a sealed missive distinguished with her mother's own seal. This, and the presence of the two servants, alarmed Willa considerably, and her eyes automatically sought Adam's. But his expression was bland and unreadable, and without further hesitation, she took the letter and opened it at once to satisfy her curiosity.

For a communication from her mother, it was surprisingly brief, but the gist of it was plain. Lady Anne had succumbed to a chest inflammation (due, doubtless, she thought, to the strain she had been subjected to of late) and felt herself at the mercy of heartless doctors and incompetent servants. She required the immediate return of Leonora to see to her care. The second page of the letter was a characteristically imperative message addressed specifically to Willa commanding her on no account to turn back from her purpose or journey, but to send Leonora back alone with the maid and footman for company so that Willa might keep their abigail for her own use. It was quite like Lady Anne to think of the details even in such an exigency.

Adam half-stood, half-sat against a table watching her as

she read the letter. She started to speak, but he suggested that it might be best if they all repaired to the private parlor, and though the coffee room was empty of patrons at this early hour, she held her tongue and followed him, the servants trailing behind her. As soon as the door was closed, she gave him the letter, which he read through at once and then handed back to her. "Most unfortunate," was his only comment.

"I suppose it is a bad cold," Willa said, trying not to sound exasperated. It was not uncommon for her mother to become ill when emotionally distressed; it had the dual felicity of excusing her from dealing with her problems directly and of eliciting comfort and concern from the members of her family. Then, struck with guilt for this unfilial thought, she said quickly, addressing the maid, "I hope it is not more?"

The young girl curtsied as she had been taught to do before speaking to the quality and said, "When we left, mistress, I wouldn't have said more ailed her ladyship than a bad case of sniffles, but her ladyship is taking it poorly, her being all on her own, and she said as how we were not to come back without Miss Leonora."

Miss Leonora, having entered the room unnoticed, took in the scene before her and then spoke. "Has Mama fallen into one of her megrims again?" She did not at all hide her exasperation. "We might have guessed there would be something, I suppose."

Willa gave her a warning glance for speaking so in front of the servants and then handed her the letter. She read it and then looked up at Willa in puzzlement. "Mama cannot be thinking," she said, still heedless of the ears of the servants. "This won't do at all; if I go back, how can you go on alone with Adam?"

Willa gave her sister a quelling look, but Adam said, at his blandest, "There is no reason why not; we are only an hour's journey from your cousins' where I escort you, and there can be no impropriety in such a short drive, accompanied by your own maid. I shall ride beside the carriage, of course, and as soon as I have seen your sister safely installed with her cousins, I shall go on at once to my own friends who expect me."

"No doubt Mama thought of that," Willa said quickly.

In spite of Adam's and Willa's efforts, Leonora looked as if she were about to speak further indiscretions. Adam, who was leaning against the unlit hearth, straightened and walked over to the footman, giving Leonora an unobtrusive warning touch on her arm as he passed. "Your journey on the mail must have been taxing," he said to the footman, handing him a coin. "It is not too early to find some refreshment in the coffee room."

When the door had closed on the pair, Willa said, "Mama must have sent them after us almost as soon as we left, for even the mail could not have beat our time by a great deal. I cannot guess what Mama is about either," she confessed. "How are you to return to town if she sent them in the mail instead of in our own carriage? I'll wager she did not have enough money about her so near the end of the quarter to give the footman enough to hire a chaise for your return."

"That is no difficulty," Adam said in an offhand way.

"If by that you mean that you shall pay for the hire, I suppose that you feel that you must and I cannot gainsay you, for it would not do at all to have to return on the common stage. But it is really too bad of Mama to put you to this trouble," she added, not hiding her annoyance. "What is worse, I fear that Nora may be right: it won't do for me to go on with you, in spite of the story you concocted for the servants."

Adam's smile was self-deprecating. "I should not like to suggest that your notions of propriety are overnice, but

Lady Anne herself, a woman of the highest moral standards, insists that you go on with me. It would be the greatest shame for us to have come so far and be so close to accomplishing our plan and have it all come to nothing."

"It is a great pity," Willa agreed, "but the purpose of Leonora coming with us at all was to give propriety to our journey. If she is gone, I fear the risk, should we ever be found out, is too great."

"What is the *greatest* pity," Leonora said, sighing heavily, "is that we have had all this tedious traveling, and more of it ahead of us, and now we shall go back to London as poor as ever we were and poorer still to come."

Though Willa could not like the idea of going on alone with Adam and staying with him at his aunt's house with no better chaperonage than her maid, she was much struck by this.

The conversation was halted at this point as the waiter brought in their breakfast, which Adam had bespoken earlier. Neither he nor Leonora said more to try to persuade Willa to go on, though in her heart Willa wished they would, for she knew that she wished to do so but could not convince herself of it.

When the covers were removed, Leonora, sighing once again, said she supposed they had best ready themselves for the return to town, and left the room. Willa remained for a moment to try to express her regret that she had brought him so far for nothing.

"In general, Mama is not inclined to ill health," she added, "but it is always possible that she is truly unwell, or perhaps it is even that she has changed her mind about this deception but did not like to say so because she feared the servants might read her letter."

He looked at her in a way that was hard to read. "I do not think Lady Anne would have expressed a wish for you to go on with me if she did not wish it," he said. "Likely it is her nerves besetting her, I know they are quite delicate at times. She must be all on edge over this despite her acquiescence."

"It is possible. Mama *is* inclined to be vaporish at times. If she is taking cold, and anxious on the top of this, it is not too surprising that she is feeling abandoned and wishes to have Nora with her, for I fear I must admit that my sister is a better comfort to her than I have ever been."

"Do you think it will help her when she discovers that nothing has been accomplished?" he suggested.

"No. I wish I knew what I should do," she said unhappily.

Adam moved his chair back farther from the table and crossed one leg over the other. "You need not do anything further," he said after a short silence. "You have come with me in good faith, and we shall consider the bargain sealed. I have already had the money paid to your Mr. Sledge—most discreetly, of course—in your name with the directions as to its disposition."

She was not looking at him, but at these words her eyes flew quickly to his. "I could not accept the money from you unearned, you know that. I suppose he has already paid Sir Nigel, so it is too late to help that, but you will have all you have given us back in full as soon as I can realize it."

"I would not accept its return," he said curtly.

"And I shall not keep it," Willa returned firmly.

"Then it shall go into a banking house or the funds in your name whether you choose to touch it or not."

Gray eyes met brown with angry willfulness, but it was the gray that dropped first.

"Very well," she said with resignation. "There is little choice for me; I shall go on with you and earn the money, for I *will* not take so much as a guinea from you that I have *not* earned."

"I beg you will not go on if you cannot like it."

"I shall like it well enough," she informed him with spirit.

"It is settled, then," he said, rising. "But if you do not wish to spend a night on the road with me, we had best leave at once."

Willa heartily concurred in this and went to her room to tell Leonora of her change in plans, and Adam was off to speak with the Drake servants and to see to the hiring of a chaise for them and Leonora to return to London in comfort.

Willa saw her sister off for town with only the protection of servants with considerable misgivings, but Leonora was quickly reconciled to her choice and assured her that she would be well. For a moment, as the chaise pulled out of the courtyard, Willa had the craven wish that she had gotten into the carriage with Leonora and was now on her way back to the metropolis and the safety of her mother's house. Which, she told herself as a means of reconciling herself to the course she was taking, would soon not be theirs at all if she were not going on to Scotland with Adam.

Their own journey began shortly after Leonora left, but not so late as to preclude their arriving at Canonbie before they were benighted. The rain of the previous night had stopped, but the sunlight of the morning gave way to an afternoon mizzle. Shortly after they stopped for the second change, Willa suggested to Adam that he might prefer to ride inside the carriage with her. She was a little shy of making the request, for as they neared their destinations, her misgivings grew, but she could not allow him to ride in the damp.

But, giving her a brief smile, he assured her that his coat was meant to weather a bit of drizzle and that he quite preferred to ride. In spite of herself, Willa could not help feeling relieved. She began to be aware of how much alone she would soon be with him, and it made her uncomfortable. It was quite one thing to talk about pretending to be his wife for a sennight, and very much another to realize that in a very short time she would really have to behave as if she were. Yet she knew that she would soon have to rid herself of her diffidence or she would never convince his aunt, be she ever so old and doddering.

Country hours were kept at Albyn Court, his aunt's house just west of Canonbie, and when they arrived at midevening, dinner was long over. While a servant went off to inform Mrs. Ramsay that her guests had arrived, another was dispatched to the kitchen to see what might be prepared to offset the hunger of Lord and "Lady" Revis, who had not stopped to eat on the road so that they might arrive at Albyn that night.

Adam led Willa across the entry hall in the wake of the butler, and as they passed through it, Willa saw that it was large and well furnished. The ceiling was vaulted, the walls were paneled in fine wood, the floor was checkered in different shades of Italian marble. When they were alone in the room, she said accusingly, "I thought you told me that your aunt lived simply in a simple manor house."

"So this is," he responded. "There are perhaps six or seven guest rooms, less than that of receiving rooms; I do not call that large. I never said it was a cottage."

Willa found the fact that the house was not what she had expected to be unsettling. She was even more unsettled when she met the imperious Maria Ramsay she had heard so much about. She had expected a frail, elderly woman, and instead she found one, far from young, but far from her dotage as well. It was clear from her slow movement as she came into the room that her health was indeed not good, but she was not so delicate that she could not come to them on her own power. After giving her nephew the most perfunctory greeting, she at once went to Willa and embraced the startled girl. "My dear," she said in a voice that was light and a bit fluty, "I could not be happier to meet you and welcome you to our family. You are not at all what I expected you to be and I could not be happier."

Willa was not sure what to make of this, but since she was thinking much the same thing in her own right, she said baldly, "Neither are you, ma'am. That is, I thought, from what Adam told me, that you were unwell."

"So I am," agreed the older woman with a surprisingly hearty laugh. "Never know from one day to the next if I'll have to keep to my bed. My damn-fool doctor told me he expected me to pop off some time ago, but I mean to live to a hundred. It's the gout mostly that does me in, but I've been eating blueberries and turnips with every meal and there is an improvement. It puts me in such a good humor that I've a mind to have a party while you're here. Can't welcome you to the family with nothing more than a handshake and a how-do-ye-do."

As Mrs. Ramsay turned away to go to a chair near the fire, Willa cast Adam an angry glance. If they were not to live quietly while they were at Albyn, the risk to her name would be much greater.

"I had Adam's note telling me you'd be here only yesterday," Mrs. Ramsay said. "You made good time, for I didn't look for you until tomorrow at the earliest. Sir Hammish Drake's girl are you? Good blood there, and sense too, if you take after your papa. I always thought that Adam would marry some silly widgeon because she was a duke's daughter and he had met her at Almack's. It seems he's got more than coats and cards in his head, after all, if he's chosen you."

The old woman's outspoken discourse nonplussed Willa, for if conversation was to be this candid for the length of their stay, she did not know how they would survive it without the truth coming out. But she soon discovered, as they left the salon and went into the dining room, that Mrs. Ramsay simply enjoyed talking and seldom required response to her monologues.

When they had eaten a simple meal, Mrs. Ramsay insisted on escorting them to their rooms herself. "I've done as you've asked, Adam," she said, ushering them into a small sitting room. "Your room is that door on the right and Willa's is on the left. But I don't hold with this modern nonsense of having separate apartments. When I married Ramsay, we shared a room and a bed for all of our days together and never once did I feel the want of privacy or have a wish to be on my own. No wonder one is forever hearing crim. con. stories. How the devil are a husband and wife to be devoted to each other if they're afraid of a little intimacy?"

"It is just a custom we prefer, Aunt," Adam said with gentle emphasis. He reached over to Willa beside him and, linking his arm in hers, pulled her closer to him. "We do not want for intimacy, I assure you." Looking down at Willa, he smiled in the way she found most irresistible. "How could it be otherwise? We are man and wife, are we not?"

It was clear from his inflection that he expected a response from her, no doubt to confirm their pretense to his aunt. She smiled back at him and said as convincingly as she could, "Yes, we are."

His smile broadened and he even laughed slightly. "Indeed we are," he concurred, and then impulsively bent his head and kissed her lightly on the lips.

Willa was too startled to respond to him, and this was no time for rebuke. She maintained her features in an amiable expression for the benefit of Mrs. Ramsay, but the moment they were left alone, she rounded on him. "If you mean to take advantage of my vulnerability in this situation, Adam," she said angrily, "I shall go to your aunt at once and inform her of this hoax and advise her to leave her money to the nearest toll collector rather than you."

He gave no sign of being chastised. "It was no big thing, Willa," he said easily. "I only kissed you, and not, you will recall, for the first time. I thought the situation called for it. I am sorry you could not like it."

"No doubt you are used to it being quite otherwise," she said darkly. "If I had thought that I could not trust you to be on your honor a gentleman, *no* consideration would have made me come here with you."

"You refine too much upon it," he said in a languid, unconcerned tone. "It was hardly the prelude to a ravishment. I might have kissed my sister so. You must learn to relax and not be forever on edge for some misbehavior on my part or suspicion on my aunt's. If you don't, you won't need to tell her we are hoaxing her; she will discern it for herself. Gout does not affect the faculties."

With this he turned and went to his own room, leaving Willa standing in the middle of the sitting room prey to mixed emotions and feeling strangely deflated. She had come this far, the deception was under way, and there was really nothing to do but to go on with it. Perhaps she was overreacting.

She went to her room to involve herself in the activity of unpacking, deciding that if she was to get through these next few days, it would be as well if she did as little examining of her feelings as possible. The door into her bedchamber was ajar when she entered and her abigail, Betsy, was already unpacking her trunk. Betsy was a young girl, near to Willa's age and generally given to chatter, but she was quiet and unusually absorbed in her work. Willa studied her curiously for a few minutes and then sat at the dressing table to remove pins from her hair. She concluded that Betsy had overheard what had passed in the sitting room between her and Adam and was shocked by it into a disapproving silence. The maid had, of necessity, been taken into her confidence before they had left London, and Willa had thought that the girl understood the nature of the business arrangement between her and Adam, but the maid's embarrassment suggested otherwise.

Willa could not like this and thought of explaining it to her again, but decided that it might only seem that she protested too much. In any case, she had not the closeness of feeling with the abigail that her sister enjoyed and this want of rapport made her feel awkward about the entire matter when discussing it with the girl. All of this only served to put Willa in mind yet again about the dangerousness of her situation and how it must look to others. She was determined to be on her guard at all times for the next few days until she was again safely returned to London.

6

The next few days took care of themselves. Willa had brought with her a number of her favorite books to wile away what she supposed would be long hours, but she found her conversations with Mrs. Ramsay both enjoyable and stimulating, for the older woman's education was as extensive as her own and her interests of equal scope. There were occasional difficult moments when Aunt Maria would hedge for details about Willa's relationship with Adam and ask forthright and embarrassing questions about their plans to set up a nursery and secure the succession. But Willa found that if she told the simple truth whenever she could with a delicate forbearance of intimate detail, she got along reasonably well. If the other woman was suspicious of her, she gave no hint of it.

The old woman's health *was* poor and only belied by her mental alertness. For much of each day she retired to her bedchamber for rest, and in these times Willa was likely to be with Adam. The day after their arrival, a neighboring squire and his wife and family came to tea, and Willa felt ready to sink with anxiety that they might possess mutual friends in England and she would thus find herself exposed. But Mrs. Ramsay was not as forthcoming in her discourses with neighbors as she was with her family, and

Adam successfully parried the visiting woman's one question into Willa's antecedents, so the visitors went away quite ignorant of her identity beyond the fact that she was Lady Revis, and Willa was able to breathe easier. Other than this one occasion, there was little threat of exposure from the outside world, for Adam had been truthful when he said his aunt lived almost reclusively. One or two of her naturalist friends, a merchant and his wife and a yeoman farmer who were involved in the movement, called, but Adam and Willa made a quick and deliberate escape when they were announced.

The faint constraint Willa had felt in Adam's company after that first night when he had kissed her, quickly vanished, and the old rapport of friendship was again between them. Living the pretense that she was his wife, from time to time she almost forgot she was not. They were just acting parts, she knew, but reflecting on it in the evenings when she was alone preparing for bed, she could not help thinking that they would hardly have gone on much differently if they were actually married. As her pleasure in his company grew, there were moments when she began to wonder if she had not made a mistake in refusing his original offer of marriage. She did not precisely admit to herself that her feelings for him might go beyond friendship, but she was aware of a desolate feeling whenever she thought about returning to London and going on as she had before, no longer so much in his company.

This was quite at odds with her original wish to be back in town as soon as possible, and forcing herself to examine her feelings, she convinced herself out of emotionalism and into good sense by telling herself not only that the life she enjoyed with him here would be quite otherwise when they were back in the world of the *ton* again, but also that there was no doubt at all that in values and aspirations they were toally unsuited to each other.

But for now she enjoyed the time they spent together. They rode daily, took long walks through the greening grounds, and even made domestic trips into Canonbie for his aunt.

On one occasion she sent them to match some embroidery thread. The town boasted a single inn, but this was a very respectable establishment, and after their purchase was made, Adam led them there to refresh themselves with lemonade and biscuits before embarking on the rattling homeward journey in his aunt's pony cart, which she had insisted they use for the short trip.

"Perhaps we should have insisted on riding," Willa agreed, listening to his droll animadversions on this mode of transportation, "but it is not so awful. I have known worse. Nora and I had a dog cart when we were children that was largely responsible for the ease with which we parted with our milk teeth."

"Well, my milk teeth are long gone," Adam retorted dryly, "and I would as soon keep the ones I have. I am very glad that you are making the best of our time here," he added after a thoughtful moment. "I supposed you would be bored to flinders or wearing yourself thin over the success of our masquerade."

"Me, bored?" Willa returned with a surprised laugh. "It is you who are a man-of-the-town. I am quite easy to entertain, and it is the incessant activity of town I usually find wearing. I am not the social creature that my mother or even Nora is."

"So you informed me," he said with a slow smile. "I believe it was when you told me we should not suit and delivered your considered opinion of my frippery nature."

Willa smiled a little sheepishly. "Ill-considered," she corrected. "I wonder you have forgiven my arrogance and self-righteousness. Yet, though we get on so well, I still think we are very different people."

"Yes, I think we are, but is it a fault?" He covered her hand with his, an intimate gesture to which she did not at all object. "In any case, let's not argue about it now. I wish nothing to mar our compatibility."

"That won't do. If we are never at loggerheads, not even your aunt will really believe us married," Willa replied.

Adam shook his head sadly. "What a deplorable opinion you have of that blessed estate. I always thought of that as the prerogative of my sex. Come," he added, rising from the table where they sat in a quiet corner of the coffee room, "we had best be returning, for I know Aunt Maria plans something special for our last night with her tonight. We shall dress in our best town finery to show our appreciation of her effort, and you will probably want to spend the afternoon with cucumber slices on your eyes or strawberries crushed on your cheeks or whatever beauty secret it is that you no doubt have for your complexion."

Willa laughed. "I should find such things a waste of good food," she told him. "My complexion owes nothing to artifice. It is what I put into my mouth, not on my face, that makes it so."

But in fact, Willa did take exceptional care with her toilet that night, more perhaps than she had done for so grand an occasion as Lady Sefton's ball. She generally wore her hair drawn back from her face, but for once she allowed Betsy to soften the style with delicate curls. The gown she wore was one which she had had made the Season before but which, because of her mourning, she had never worn. It was of a golden-colored satin that caught the light and gave the gown the twinkling depths of a glittering topaz.

Willa might disdain the women who lived for fashion, but she was not at all impervious to the exultation of knowing that she looked her very best. The color in her cheeks owed no more to the rouge pot than her complexion did to cucumbers or strawberries; she appeared the blushing bride, indeed.

Adam's admiration of her efforts was apparent, and during their dinner Mrs. Ramsay remarked several times how well they looked together, making Willa color all the more. After dinner Willa played the pianoforte, and making the effort to extend her hospitality on their last night, the old woman did not retire early to bed as was her custom but stayed to engage them in a game of three-handed whist that more often resulted in laughter than serious play.

By town standards, it was a dull evening, but Willa enjoyed herself and thought it came to an end all too soon. Generally she retired shortly after the older woman, and before Adam, who was used to later hours, but tonight Willa lingered, and when he invited her to join him in the library to share a glass of brandy with him, she accepted, though she did not really care for spirits.

She made herself comfortable in the corner of a sofa near the fire, for the night was chill, and accepted the glass offered to her. Her first sip of the liquid was searing, but a second was easier and a third convinced her of his assertion that its texture was smooth.

"Mama would never have given me permission to come with you had she guessed that you meant to ply me with strong spirits," she admonished, accepting a bit more from him.

He gave her one of his more enigmatic smiles and replaced the stopper in the decanter. He sat near her in an adjacent chair. "When a man of honor conducts a seduction—and that is not a contradiction of terms," he informed her, "he relies on his charm and wit to accomplish the thing.

Only base libertines use artificial means to attain a nefarious end."

Willa, mellowed by the pleasantness of the evening and the warmth of the brandy, found nothing alarming in his quizzing her so. She laughed. "Does this mean that my virtue is safe, or that you are a libertine?"

"It means that I have great faith in my mastery of my baser nature," he said in a flat, dry way, "which, let me tell you, is at this moment doing all it can to convince me that honor is a set of rules for cold fish. Nobility, at least at this level of the bottle, is winning out, so fear not, fair lady."

"Should I take the decanter with me to my room or simply lock my door tonight?"

"The door to your room doesn't lock," he said succinctly.

Willa opened her eyes at him. "How do you know that, Adam?" she said awfully. She studied him for a moment and then said half-seriously, "*Are* you trying to seduce me?"

His responding smile was small and slow to form. "Most women would be insulted if the attempt were not made," he said softly, but still in a light vein that she might read as she chose.

"I am not most women."

"I know that well," he said with sudden gravity. "Perhaps that is one of the things that makes me want you so very much."

Willa caught her breath, but spoke coolly, determined not to let him see that he had disconcerted her. "A poor reason."

"Is there *any* reason you find adequate?" he asked a trace caustically. He saw the flash of defensive anger come into her eyes and said quickly, "I won't quarrel with you, Willa; I would rather love you instead."

To her dismay, he rose and sat beside her on the small

sofa, and the movement required to bring her into his arms was equally small. She supposed it was the brandy, but she felt a strange lethargy that made her unwilling to resist. He took her face in his hands and raised it to kiss.

At first his lips on hers were as light as they had been when he had kissed her the day they had arrived, but in a moment the kiss deepened and he embraced her fully. Willa did not fight him or try to push him away. She allowed the surge of anticipation to sweep over her, and could actually feel her pulse increase. She could not deny the attraction he held for her, and for this brief moment neither could she resist giving into it.

He did not press the advantage her clear response gave him, but instead, he brought the embrace to an end and moved slightly back from her in a deliberate way, as if he found it necessary. When Willa opened her eyes and looked into his, his pupils were wide and his eyes looked black in the soft candlelight. "What are you feeling?" he asked softly.

"That I wish you would do it again," something made her reply with disastrous honesty before she could guard her tongue. He needed little encouragement, and once again she found herself wrapped in his strong arms as greedily searching his mouth and lips as he did hers.

Where this might have led was in the realm of half-admitted fantasy. For a few precious minutes she gave in to her desires, tasting the sweet fruit that she had so long denied herself. The wistfulness that had plagued her for the last few days became genuine longing. She was very close to succumbing to him and the urgings of her own body, which refused to heed her mind and conscience. Gathering together all her resources, she managed to pull away from him at last and he made no effort to physically restrain her. But his next words and the tone of his voice were nearly as seductive as his touch and his lips. "Come to me, Willa," he said, his voice soft and thick with desire. "I promise you won't regret it."

It would have been so easy to fall back into his arms, her own longings satisfied, her uncertain future settled at last, but she could not. Even in the face of such overwhelming temptation, she could not but believe that today's joys would be paid for with tomorrow's unhappiness when their passion for each other was spent. Then their incompatibilities must surface, and her heart told her that the pain she would feel then would be far worse than should she wrench herself from him now. Tears formed in her eyes, but she blinked them away. Sadly, she shook her head.

"Damn!" he said with great abruptness, and rose to walk a little away from her, as if he would no longer bear her closeness. He turned back to face her and stared at her long enough to make her uncomfortable. His expression was completely shuttered.

"You know my convictions are not lightly held, Adam," she said quietly when the silence became unbearable.

"Oh, I know that very well," he said acidly. "They are just held stubbornly." He let out his breath as if he had been holding it, and sat down again, but in the chair, not in the sofa. "I don't think I am a vain man," he said, and there was nothing of the languid Corinthian in his voice when he spoke, "but I never supposed I would have to beg the woman of my choice to marry me."

"Please don't," Willa said with alarm.

His expression could never be hard for long, and a small laugh softened it now. "I won't. But I want you to admit, at least to yourself, that there is more between us than mere liking. If you will not come to me now, at least be open to what is between us. At least give me permission to prove to you that there are not the differences between us that you imagine there to be."

Willa rose from the sofa, feeling light-headed, which she blamed completely on the brandy. "I don't know what I think," she said in a confused way.

He reached up and possessed himself of her hand. "I mean to prove to you that we are a perfect mating."

She found that looking into his eyes while he touched her even in so perfunctory a way was more than she could bear. She could not trust herself to speak, so she only nodded, letting him attach what meaning he would to the gesture. He dropped her hand and in a disjointed way she bid him good night and went up to her room.

The next morning Willa's cheeks felt warm whenever she thought of the abandoned way she had responded to his embrace, and the thought of meeting him alone over the breakfast table was discomforting. But, for once, Mrs. Ramsay did not take her tray in her room and made a comfortable third in the breakfast room. Willa was still a bit shy of meeting Adam's eyes at first, but his manner toward her was light and friendly, and by the time their meal was done, her constraint had dissipated.

Almost as soon as they had eaten and seen to any last-minute packing, the carriage was brought around for them to be off at an early start. The weather was once again fine and he elected to ride beside the carriage as he had on the journey northward. When the weather broke on the third day and dark clouds became a downpour, he had to give up riding for the confines of the carriage. He was an entertaining companion, and when the day was too dim for them to read to each other or play chess on a traveling set he had brought along, they conversed with the ease of old friends.

Even the nights that they spent on the road—in lesser-known inns this time, to avoid possible acquaintances—were not discomfiting, and it was not until she was alone in bed that she allowed herself to succumb to her thoughts on all that had happened between them since that day when he had asked her to be his wife.

If nothing else, the specter of ruin was at bay. By now Sir Nigel had returned to town and received Mr. Sledge's message to call upon him. Even her everyday life and her family's would be somewhat improved by the income from the generous sum he had settled on her in the funds. They had successfully duped his aunt with their pretense (though now that she knew and liked Mrs. Ramsay, she could not think of the part she had played without some feeling of guilt despite the old woman's high-handedness), and now that they were so nearly safely home, it seemed apparent that they had averted any possible scandal by being seen alone together by someone who would know them.

The only difficulty that remained was sorting out her own jumbled emotions. After what had happened that last night in Scotland, she could no longer be positive that what she had assumed to be simple liking and physical attraction was not something more. But she could not believe in a future harmony for them, and with all her heart she did not want to be in love with him, for then what peace would she have with him or without him?

The last day on the road seemed the longest to her, and when their carriage at last pulled up in front of the house in Cavendish Square, Willa was glad that their enforced intimacy was at an end so that some distance between them might give her time to think.

Adam insisted on escorting her into the house, sending his carriage on and declaring that he would be glad of the short walk to his own house to stretch his legs after so long a ride. Both Lady Anne and Leonora bustled into the front hall to greet them. After kissing her sister, who reached her first, Willa found herself in an unexpected embrace from her mother, who was not usually demonstrative.

"Good heavens, Mama," Willa said, laughing as she

caught her breath. "One would think I had been gone a twelvemonth instead of a fortnight."

"What an unnatural parent I would be if I did not miss my firstborn were she gone a day from the shelter of my bosom!" exclaimed her mother effusively.

Willa allowed herself to be led into one of the saloons on the ground floor, where light refreshment was already laid out in anticipation of their arrival. They were followed by Adam and Leonora, who seemed to be having an animated conversation of their own.

"You must tell me *everything*," Lady Anne said to her elder daughter the moment the door was closed. "I have been on pins the whole day waiting to behold you."

Willa was so surprised by the excess of this speech that she did not notice the quelling frown that Leonora cast her mother. "I think it would be best, Mama, if we allowed Willa to go to her room to refresh herself," Leonora said, "before you begin quizzing her."

Though Willa looked forward to ridding herself of the dirt of travel, she was in no great hurry to go up to her room to change. "Actually," she said, addressing her mother, "the entire trip passed very pleasantly. All went quite well and I don't believe Mrs. Ramsay ever suspected that I was not what I claimed to be, though I own I was uncomfortable accepting her kindness knowing I was deceiving her. But I am glad to be back. We were up with the dawn today to be certain that we would be home tonight before dark."

Lady Anne seemed barely to listen to her. "I own myself surprised that you were in such a hurry to bring your idyl to an end," she said with an arch smile. "You might have spent another week in Scotland with my blessing only sending a note so that we should not fret over you.

"Without Nora to give us countenance," Adam said in a pointed way, "it was best not to court indiscretion."

"That can hardly matter now," the dowager said dismis
sively, blithely ignoring the warning in Adam's voice o
the searing looks cast her by her younger daughter.

But Willa had noted both and was at a loss to under
stand. Only one thing was clear to her; something wa
afoot to which she was not privy. "Why shouldn't it mat
ter, Mama?" she asked with an air of casualness.

Lady Anne smiled broadly. "You needn't be coy with
me, miss. Didn't Adam tell you I knew the whole of hi
plan before ever you started on your journey? He is a sly
one, is he not? It sadly piqued my poor mother's heart to
have my firstborn wed without a proper bestowal before al
of our friends, but I have decided that we shall have a
grand ball to make the announcement when we are out o
mourning at the end of the month. It will be the event o
the Season and make Maria Sefton's ball look like a frip
pery rout."

Willa listened to her mother in some confusion, he
brows drawn together. The words were clear enough to
understand, but she could not believe that she compre
hended them correctly. "What are you saying, Mama.
You know perfectly that Adam and I only pretended to be
married to convince his aunt to leave him his grandfather'
fortune."

Lady Anne stared at her with eyes that became round
and then she turned swiftly in her chair to where Adam
stood near the window, propping the wall with his shoul
ders. "Libertine," she cried out dramatically. "You have
deceived a mother's trust. We are not so without protec
tors that you will not answer for this."

Willa's penetrating gaze searched Adam's face for some
answer to what she was hearing, but his hooded eyes
looked away from her. Leonora gamely jumped into the
fray to say that her mother was doubtless feeling light
headed from her recent cold and should perhaps lie down

but Lady Anne ignored her and demanded an answer from the young man, who was the focus of all eyes in the room.

With the sangfroid for which he was noted, he righted himself and calmly walked over to the table, where wine and glasses were placed, and carefully poured out a glass, sipping the contents before answering. His eyes, when they at last met Willa's, held no disquietude and, if anything, seemed self-mocking. "Forgive me, Willa." It was half-question and half-statement. He raised his glass to her slightly and drank it down.

"Why should I need to forgive you?" Willa asked, her voice dark with suspicion.

"You would certainly have had to have the truth eventually," he said, putting down his empty glass on the table and coming nearer to her. "It would seem it must be now."

"That would be best," Willa said. "I feel I am the victim of a conspiracy and I would like it explained to me at once. Is there something you would wish to say to me, Mama?" she asked, turning to her parent, who, after arguing briefly with Leonora, had subsided into a petulant silence.

But Lady Anne would not meet her gaze levelly. "Let Adam tell you. It is he who has deceived us both and has made this mess."

Willa looked up at him again and he responded with one of his lazy smiles. "I did keep my word," he said first to Lady Anne. Then, turning to Willa, he said, "When your mother greeted you so effusively today, she believed she was welcoming you home not as a maiden daughter but as a married woman. I spoke to her about my plan to take you to Scotland before you did, and I told her that by the time we returned it would be as my wife. It was the reason you found her so agreeable to my plan."

Willa could scarcely credit her ears. "But you knew I

would not marry you. How could you expect that a fortnight would change my mind?"

"Conceit, I expect," he said with a small self-mocking
laugh. "It may be that, but I have long believed you are
not indifferent to me. I thought . . . Well, it doesn't matter
what I thought now. The point is that I hoped that away
from town I might convince you that I am not the shallow
social creature you condemn me to be. Even Nora knew
nothing of it until she received your mother's letter and I
took her into my confidence before she left so that she
would not be concerned about leaving you alone with me.

"Her removal was your mother's embellishment; she
hoped that an enforced *tête-à-tête* would hurry our intimacy along, which Nora told me in a letter I received the
same day you received her message that your mother was
not seriously ill." He paused for a reaction to this information, but there was none even from Willa, who regarded
him grimly. The look he gave her was decidedly whimsical.
"But my vanity did outpass the strength of my attractions.
That last night at Albyn . . . I won't distress you with the
memory now. I really believed you would come to me. I
am quite humbled, but that won't remedy what is done.
That is what I wish you to forgive me."

Before Willa could respond to this, Lady Anne said
impatiently, "Well, did you do the thing or not?"

Adam did not even bother to glance her way. "For
better or for worse, my dear Willa, willing or unwilling,
you are my wife."

Very calmly and very quietly, Willa said, "How is that
possible?"

"Marriage by consent. In Scotland, it is all that is required."

"I have never heard of such a thing," Willa said, still
bemused. "In any case, I have never consented to be your
wife."

The corners of his mouth lifted almost imperceptibly.

"The phrase is perhaps a bit deceptive. In Scotland most of the formalities of tying the knot are dispensed with if one so wishes, which is what makes it such a popular destination for eloping couples. In fact, all that is really required is that a man and woman declare themselves to be man and wife before a witness, or even without one if they later admit it to a third party. It is a delicate business, so I took care to have not only my Aunt Maria hear me proclaim us married and you concur, but your own maid as well, for the door to your bedchamber was ajar and I heard her clearly inside moving about as she unpacked your trunks. I am sure our voices carried."

Willa, who had excellent recall, had no difficulty placing the scene he described, but she did not wish to accept what he told her. "This is nonsense," she said. "I know we said some such thing to your aunt, but I cannot believe that in our modern times such a barbaric custom could still exist."

"That would not have been the adjective of my choice to describe the law," Adam said meditatively, "but I assure you that it is still valid. I did not leave it to chance, you know, but made sure of it the next morning after I proposed the plan to you."

"I cannot believe you would do such a thing and my own mother abet you," she said, appalled. "The marriage may be valid in Scotland, but is it recognized here? I have heard of the wedding chapels that dot the border for the benefit of eloping couples and presumably some sort of ceremony takes place. Why would this be necessary if the custom you claim were recognized here?"

"I haven't the least idea," he admitted, "but I know you are my wife not only in Scotland but here as well. You need not trust my word; discreet inquiry will give you the truth of the matter as it did me."

Willa had to believe him. He was not a fool to make up

such a fantastic tale if it could be given the lie. But how could she readily accept what he was saying to her? It was unthinkable to imagine that she had been used in such a way by people she had trusted.

Lady Anne, who had thoughtfully remained quiet during this exchange, said at last, "It is a bit irregular, not quite the thing, perhaps, but we need not puff off how the thing was accomplished. A simple announcement in the *Post*, I think, will suffice."

Adam turned and looked at her with faint surprise, as if he had forgotten her presence. "I think Willa and I might deal better in this matter if left to ourselves," he suggested gently.

"We shall not deal at all," Willa retorted. "I cannot believe you would suppose that I would accept this high-handed ordering of my life. I cannot, I *will* not." Her anger rose to supplant her confusion and she was quite willing to give it rein.

Lady Anne rose and made a breif signal to her wide-eyed younger daughter to do the same. "Adam's method may have been high-handed, but it is foolish to cavil at the result," she advised Willa. "You know perfectly well that you have always liked Adam very much and I have always believed it was really far and above that with you. Now, instead of worrying about a ragtag existence, not only is your future settled, but ours as well, for Adam has agreed to drawing up settlements and is most generous."

"Dear Lord," said Willa on a breath as the thought struck her, "I have, after all, been sold."

"You will do yourself no good enacting Cheltenham tragedies, my girl," her mother advised her as she walked around her chair toward the door. "Gentlemen dislike melodrama, you know."

Willa turned her wrath on her parent, who had aided in the duplicity. "Disabuse yourself of the notion that this marriage is valid, Mama, or that I have any intention of falling in with your plans for me."

Half-pushing a reluctant Leonora out the door ahead of her, Lady Anne bestowed a condescending, cat-in-the-cream-pot smile on her daughter. "My dear," she said infuriatingly, "what else is there to do?" She went out and closed the door behind her with a sharp little click.

"If it *is* valid," Willa said with icy intent to Adam, "and I by no means concede it, it will be annulled at once."

He arranged himself in the chair that Lady Anne had vacated. He slouched a bit in a negligent way, but his eyes met hers squarely. "I am sorry, Willa. I did not mean for it to be like this."

"And how did you mean it to be?" she rejoined hotly.

He sighed. "I'd hoped to change your mind about me. I thought I'd be able to convince you to accept my offer before we left Aunt Maria, and then it would not have mattered so much that I had done the thing out of hand. I even thought you might not mind overmuch being swept off your feet, for it came to me that you advised someone to that course once."

She looked at him incredulous. "A man of your rank, person, and fortune could not be so desperate for a wife that you would wish for one who is unwilling. Can that inheritance have mattered so much to you?"

"It mattered not at all," he said. "I admit to my vanity and arrogance. What else can I do? When you pushed me away that last night, I knew I had failed, but the thing could not be undone."

"It will be undone."

He stood up. "I married you, Willa, for the same reason I first asked you to be my wife: I have been in love with you these six months, and likely more without realizing it. I truly convinced myself that you cared for me but feared the fate that befell your parents, who were certainly mismatched." His voice was level, and after a pause, when he spoke again, it had taken on a harder quality. "You shall have the annulment if that is what you wish."

Willa stared up at him. It was what she wanted, but somehow she could not now find the words to repeat her demand. But he clearly found this unnecessary; he gave her a brief nod, looking, she thought, as discomposed as she had ever seen him, and quit the room.

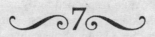

When Adam entered the front hall to retrieve his hat, he paused at the table beside the foot of the stairs where it reposed. He thought he heard a sound above him and looked up the stairs to find Leonora beckoning to him at the top. Her eyes darted warily and her motion calling to him was definitely stagy. Here indeed he was in the midst of melodrama. His ready humor, capable of surfacing even during his blackest moments, came to the fore and the severe lines his features had been set in when he left Willa relaxed.

He obeyed the summons and went up the stairs to follow Leonora into the morning room, where he found Lady Anne waiting for him. His mouth tightened again at the sight of her, for she had precipitated him into the unhappy position in which he now found himself.

"I don't suppose you were able to talk her into her senses," the dowager said without preamble. "She is a stubborn girl, so very like Sir Hammish—all principles and philosophies and not a bit of practicality to be had. Never fear, though, she shall come around. You may safely leave it to me."

She handed him a glass of Madeira which she had already poured out for him, and he readily took this as well as the chair she indicated. "But I don't think I shall," he said as he settled himself. "Would you think my sensibilities too refined if I said I should rather be a part of her principles than her practicality? If you mean to badger her into having me, you do me no favor."

"It seems to me that you have not done so very well on your own," Lady Anne responded tartly.

"Quite a nice Madeira," he said, inspecting the wine in the glass he held. "Sir Hammish was almost as renowned for his palate as he was for his poems. I take it you did not have my note, which I sent on ahead of us by special messenger?" he added with an abruptness that startled his hostess.

She bent on him a look that would have dampened a lesser man, but that appeared not to affect him at all. "Your note was not at all to the point," she said haughtily.

"I did not think my periods at all oblique," he said, regarding her over the rim of his glass. "I told you that all was not as we planned and to say nothing of your expectation until we had had the time to confer. Is that what you misunderstood?"

There was a faint sarcastic inflection to his tone, and though he appeared calm, Lady Anne sensed that he was really quite angry. But she was not a woman to admit a fault. "You are insolent, my lord, and I do not tolerate that, even in a son."

"Which, unhappily at this moment, I am not."

Lady Anne's face fell. "You said the marriage, however odd, was valid," she cried accusingly.

"No marriage is valid that has not been consummated," he said, speaking plainly. "An annulment is merely a necessary formality,"

"Oh, Mama," Leonora said miserably from her perch on the wide sill of a window, "why could you not have trusted Adam and said nothing until he had spoken? Now Willa has set up her back and will probably never have nim, and whatever she may have said about not wishing to be married, I know that she cares for Adam." She saw Adam turn to her sharply, and added, "Of all of our friends she has always liked you best."

"She is in a pet now," Lady Anne said. "As soon as she is over it, you may depend on me to show her where her duty lies."

"No." Adam did not raise his voice, but the word was a clear command. "I don't want her to be my wife because she is bullied in to it. If she comes to me, it will be of her choosing or *I* shall not have her."

"Whatever your shortcomings, Revis, I never supposed you would be an inept lover. You spend a fortnight virtually alone with a green girl who is already disposed toward you and you could not manage a simple seduction."

"Mama!"

Adam's eyes narrowed in a way that his friends would have described as dangerous. "I might have managed it, but I have told you I prefer a willing mate."

"I wasn't suggesting rape," Lady Anne said defensively.

"Mama!"

"Oh, hush, girl. Adam knows well enough what I mean. Under the circumstances—"

"Under the circumstances," he said levelly, "I felt more bound than ever to behave toward Willa honorably."

The censure in his words was clear to her, but Lady Anne did not see that she deserved it. She was as steadfast as any mother at guarding her daughters. Virtue, which was after all a marketable quality, must be protected. But in her mind, Willa's marriage to Adam was a settled thing, whatever this nonsense they were spouting now about annulments. The fine points of honor were to her mere fastidiousness. "Young men in my day," she said roundly, "did not choose to refine on their feelings so greatly. But of course, it must be as you see fit, though there would not be all this foolish talk today if you had not been quite so nice."

"Adam knows better, if you do not, Mama," Leonora said, her cheeks rosy. "Willa digs in her heels when she is pushed."

"Who said anything about pushing? Willa is a sensible girl, as are you, for I have raised you both to be that way. If she knew herself to be Adam's wife and no hope for it, she would come around soon enough, you may depend upon it."

At last seeking out her room to change, Willa did so with great rapidity and then dismissed a yawning Betsy. She had whipped herself into a fine state of fury. The eyes that looked back at her from her mirror as she brushed out her hair sparked; her breasts rose and fell with her quick breaths. She cast down her brush and paced angrily the length of the room. Betsy dared to comment on her highly emotional state while she unpacked Willa's trunk only to be sent from the room with a sharp word, a rare thing for her to receive from her generally soft-spoken mistress. Returning to the servants' hall feeling much ill used, she declared to all assembled there that Miss Drake was in a rare taking, and encouraged by the handsome new under-footman to vent her injured feelings a bit later as they shared a cup of tea, she animadverted at some length on the character of Miss Drake comparing it unfavorably with that of her favorite, Miss Leonora.

Willa, for her part, was feeling guilty for having been so sharp with the abigail. She had needed to lash out at someone, and Betsy, whom she occasionally found to be impertinent, had been there. Her fury was rapidly cooling, only to be replaced by a sense of profound unhappiness. Willa did not wish to call the maid back again, and she was forced to pull awkwardly at the small buttons at the back of her gray tweed traveling dress. The thing was at last accomplished, but not without snapping a few threads and snagging a fingernail in the process.

Half-undressed, Willa flopped down on her bed; it seemed all of a piece to her today and she could not remember feeling so sore-set since the day her father had died.

At first she tried to convince herself that it was caused by the disappointment she felt at having been so grossly deceived by the people she had trusted most in the world; then she wished to believe that it was due to the outrage she felt at having been a victim of Adam's unbridled arrogance. She simply refused to think of the finality with which she had dismissed Adam Revis from her life, because of the emptiness this made her feel.

When both anger and self-pity were spent, she got up off the bed and walked over to her dressing table. She stared dispassionately at her features, which seemed pale and drawn. "You shall end an ape leader and deserve it," she said aloud to the washed-out young woman who faced her, and then was a little at a loss to understand why she had done so.

But she had herself in hand now and she finished undressing at a calmer and more successful rate and soon sat before her mirror, again dabbing lavender water on her face. But as she worked this time, she did not meet her eyes reflected back to her in the mirror.

Willa did not go down to dinner that night, nor would she take a tray in her room. She was exhausted both emotionally and physically, but when she retired early to bed, she found that her mind would not obey her body, and unbidden thoughts tumbled about in her mind, making sleep impossible.

Some of these thoughts did not bear examining. Anger was an easier emotion to deal with, so she dwelt on the outrageous way that she had been used and came to the conclusion that if she had the means of repaying Adam, it would give her immense satisfaction to be able to throw in his face the money he had given her to pay Sir Nigel. She would return the amount he had put into the funds for her, of that there was no doubt, but how she was ever to realize an additional ten thousand pounds, she could not even begin to think. If she sold their house and possessions to satisfy her pride and sense of ill usage, she would be casting herself, Leonora, and their mother into the very ruin she had thought to save them from. It was not to be considered. Unhappily she knew she would have to be content to return the half, but she meant to pay him the rest, if it took her the rest of her life.

She had at last almost drifted into sleep when a sudden thought occurred. She must think again of starting her school; without the income from the amount Adam had settled on her, they would in any case need additional income, and surely once the school was established she would be able to set a portion of her profits aside to rid herself all the more quickly of her hated debt to Lord Revis. By the time she finally fell asleep, she had convinced herself of the success of her scheme and imagined a very satisfying scene featuring herself returning the ten thousand pounds to an abashed Adam.

As early the next morning as she could, she called on Mr. Sledge. Without commenting on how he had received the money—he was ever a man of discretion—he assured her that he had called upon Sir Nigel and retrieved her father's bills and vouchers; and, yes, a similar amount had been invested in the funds in her name.

Without so much as the twitch of an eye muscle did he betray any emotion when she told him that the latter was to be liquidated at once and paid to Lord Revis, and though Willa knew from the extreme correctness of his manner that he did not at all like her notion of starting chool, he agreed to look into how one would go about the matter at once. To be sure that he did so and would not hope that she would forget the matter, she informed him pointedly that she would call again in a sennight to see what he had discovered.

The matter of her father's debts settled in such a clear way, Willa did not expect to see Sir Nigel again any time soon except in company. She was quite startled, then, when very shortly after she had returned from her interview with the solicitor, Sir Nigel came into the back parlor where she sat alone sorting embroidery silks, quite unannounced. As he entered, she looked up, and caught her breath in surprise.

His smile seemed mocking. "I beg your pardon, Willa, for coming upon you so," he said, still advancing toward her. She stood suddenly, seeming almost prepared for flight, and he abruptly stopped his progress into the room. "Have I fallen so low in your estimation that you need to fear my person?"

"How is it that Biddle did not announce you?" she asked with no welcome in her voice.

"You have a new footman and I was able to convince him that the length and depth of my friendship with you and your dear mother made ceremony quite unnecessary."

"I am not surprised that your eloquence succeeded," she replied with a small sneer. "Even well-paid servants are relatively poor." She resumed her chair but did not ask him to sit. "I cannot think what you can have to say to me. I am informed by Mr. Sledge that the business between us is settled."

Without her permission, he pulled out a chair from the other side of the table where she worked, and sat down, He gave no appearance at all of a man unsure of his welcome. "My dear, I am here because I made certain that you would have something that you wished to say to *me*."

"I? I think my actions spoke clearly enough. But, if you wish it." She carefully and deliberately pushed aside the silks, and folding her hands before her on the table, she looked at him levelly. "Sir Nigel, I do not thank you or feel myself honored that you wished to force me to be your mistress. The complete truth is this: I would not have had you had it been the only means of saving myself from the Fleet. Is that clear enough, sir?"

He flinched at neither her words nor her hard tone. His mobile brows rose slightly. "Why, not at all! You misunderstood my intention, I assure you. In the matter of your father's debts, it was purely a business transaction between friends. I only meant that the degree of friendship must affect the outcome of any business."

Willa inclined her head slightly. "As you say. I think the matter was handled exactly in accordance with the degree of our friendship."

"As *you* wish," he said, smiling. "I confess that what does bring me here is my sad disposition to curiosity. I cannot but recall that on the day we first discussed the matter, you feared that you would not easily realize the amount of the debt. I had the felicity of meeting your dear mama from time to time while you were visiting friends—in Yorkshire, was it not?—and she made no mention to me of receiving an unexpected largess. In fact, it occurs to me that she was equally unaware of any debt. Can it be that you did not take her into your confidence?"

"Surely your concern in the matter ended with the payment you received?" she said sweetly, and began to gather up her silks, intending to bring this interview to an end even if it meant walking out and leaving him to find his way out. "It is really not proper for me to receive you with Mama and Nora from home. If you will excuse me, I shall ask you to leave now."

But he was not to be easily snubbed. He smiled again in

a way that she frankly disliked. "It is a curious thing, is it not, that Lord Revis was gone from town for about the same period that you were visiting your friends."

"No doubt Lord Revis pleases himself in such matters."

"No doubt," he agreed, and added in a silky tone, "I saw your mama last night when she popped in for a few minutes at Sally Jersey's musical party. That was how I was made aware that you were returned. I also saw Adam Revis going into his house late yesterday afternoon, so I knew that he too was among us again. I mentioned this to your mother last night and she seemed much struck by the coincidence, almost disconcerted, one might have said."

Willa began to put the silks away and did not look at him as she spoke. "It would be an odd thing if Lord Revis informed Mama of his comings and goings." She started to rise to leave, but his next words aborted the action and caused her a surge of anxiety that made her heart beat faster.

"And did she also not know that the carriage in which you left for Yorkshire—or was it Scotland? I quite forget— had Revis' crest upon the panel?"

There was no mistaking the insinuation. Willa's temper flared at his insolence, but she did not wish to cross swords with him in such a dangerous game. He could not be more than guessing, and she could not even imagine how it was he knew so much. "Lord Revis is a generous friend," she said dampeningly.

"And you, Willa? Are you also generous to him?"

Acting almost without thought, Willa reached across the narrow worktable and struck him full in the face. The imprint of her hand was clear on his cheek, but he sat with his smile still in place as if nothing at all had happened.

"Don't play me for a fool, girl," he said quite amiably. "I was not to your fancy, but Revis was. I suppose I should retreat from the ranks gracefully—a lady has the right to her choice, I suppose—but I dislike the manner in which I was given my congé. Instead of telling me honestly that you were in another man's protection, you let me dangle for a fortnight and then left me to a demeaning meeting with your underling. Did you and Revis laugh over it on your journey? It was a double victory, was it not? You duped an old woman and scorned an old fool, did you not?"

Willa saw at once that there was little point in trying to bluff her way through this; his information was clearly much more than an informed guess. "I do not know what you think you know," she said, managing not to let her agitation show in her voice, "but you seem to have pieced together a deal of misinformation."

He laughed softly. "No, I have not. My source is excellent and the facts clear. Don't you know never to take a servant completely into your confidence? Especially a pretty maid with an eye for a well-turned leg and shoulders finely set in a livery coat."

He had to mean Betsy. It was unthinkable that she would have betrayed the family she had been with since childhood, but it must be true. She said nothing, but her thoughts were not hard to read.

"You must not blame her too much," he advised. "She thought her confidences safe enough; how was she to know that your new footman is brother to my valet?" He laughed at her outraged expression. "Oh, it is the meerest coincidence, I assure you; I am not so Machiavellian."

"You are abominable," Willa said in a wondering way. "You don't even care for the welfare of your informant, for you must know that I shall dismiss him at once."

"You mistake my character again," he said, sounding wounded. He picked up a skein of blue thread that had fallen out of the basket beside Willa and began to unravel it. "It is just that, whether I win or lose the hand, I prefer

o have all the cards turned up at the end. And I am loyal
o those who are loyal to me, as you would have discovered, my dear Willa, if you had not played fast and loose
vith me."

"What do you mean to do with your information?"
Willa asked him baldly.

"That depends on you."

His tone was so insinuating that Willa blanched. She
stood abruptly. She snatched the thread from his fingers
and said in a voice of ice, "I want you to leave. At once."

"When I have said this, and not before. If you wish to
make a scene, it is all one to me. You don't? Good. Why
don't you sit, my dear? I shall have to stand too if you
continue to do so, and it is always so awkward to discuss
matters of moment in that position."

Willa sat again without demur.

"It seems to me that I have the advantage of you, dear
girl. Now that I have made you aware that I am not the
fool you took me for, I could wish you well of Revis and
wash my hands of you, or I could use what I know to my
own best advantage." He paused and regarded her for a
long moment in a way that made her feel like a mare on
Tattersall's auction block. "If you were me, my dear,
lovely Ice Maiden, which would you do?"

"I would leave you in peace to get on with your life,
having disrupted it quite enough already," she replied with
alacrity.

He smiled broadly. "But then you are not me. What a
tidbit this would make for the dowagers to whisper over
on a dull Friday at Almack's."

Willa felt a cold chill run through her. "I cannot stop
you if that is your intention."

"Yes you can. On the whole, I am not a man to gladly
take another's leavings, but in your case, I mean to make
an exception. We shall pretend that the past three weeks

have not taken place and it is the day after I first offered to make you mine, and you, having spent the night before weighing the advantages of my generosity, are meeting me now to express your delight and acceptance."

"You know I never would."

His brows shot upward. "Are you quite certain that you have the stomach for complete and absolute ruin? The mud will splatter your mother and sister as well, you know that. Once again, my dear, I fear you are about to be hasty. I do not mean to give you a third opportunity to rethink your answer."

Willa knew that he meant it. She also knew that he spoke the truth; a ruin more complete than any her father's debts could bring them was inevitable. There was only one response she could make to him, and though it was as nearly unpalatable to her as was his insulting offer, she had to do so; all choice had been removed.

"If you listen to the gossip of servants, you will find yourself looking quite foolish, Sir Nigel. As Lady Revis, I think my credit in the world can withstand the spite of one loose fish."

His short laugh was condescending. "Lady Revis? My good girl, surely you are being, shall we say, optimistic?"

Even aware of the enormity of the step she had just taken, she was able to feel immense satisfaction on being able to return his smile and say sweetly, "No, merely discreet. It is not to be announced yet, for Mama insists on the strictest mourning period being observed for Papa. Yet I shall make you a present of the news: Adam and I are already wed. The journey into which you have read so much on the word of a reprimanded servant was in the nature of a wedding trip."

It was quite obvious that she had nonplussed him. He blinked and looked at her in quite a strange way for such a time that she knew he was trying to decide whether or not to believe her. Finally he took a deep breath, and his expression lost all trace of arrogant confidence and was almost sheepish. "What can I say to you, dear girl? I must believe you, of course. You would not be foolish enough to fob me off with a lie so easily discovered." He stood. "I have behaved badly, but I was clearly mistaken in my assumptions. I would most abjectly apologize for my behavior, but I expect it would not be enough." This last was said with an air of hopefulness, but she continued to regard him with immobile features. "I thought not. I wish you might have told me about you and Revis from the beginning. We should both have been saved some chagrin."

"I do not feel that way."

"No. It is I who have made a complete ass of myself." He had brought his hat and stick into the room with him; now he gathered these up and made her a brief bow. But as if with afterthought he turned to her again and said, "I am a man of occasionally unguarded passions. This time they clearly ran away with me. You probably won't think this a compliment, but it is your loveliness, your tantalizing aloofness that had made it so. For what it is worth, please know that you would never have come to harm of me."

"You can hardly expect me to believe that," she said stonily.

"Must this forever stand between us, Willa? We must meet, after all. It will be wondered at if your mama receives me and you do not."

After a moment Willa said, "That is true. But I think it would be best if our 'friendliness' in future was marked by a decided distance. You no doubt realize, since he has not called upon you himself, that I have not taken Adam into my confidence in this matter. I thought it would create exactly the difficulties that we both wish to avoid. However, you have my word that I shall do so at once if you attempt any manner of intimacy toward me again."

He spread his hands palm upward in a gesture of submission. "I am your obedient, fair lady. What can I do but comply?" His air was rueful. "I truly wish you and Revis well of each other," he said, and left her.

Willa could have wept for a combination of relief and frustration. On the one hand, she was free from the unwanted advances of Sir Nigel for good; on the other, she had made a decision that must affect the rest of her life.

She hardly knew what impulse had led her to it. But she feared that there had been more to her admission of the marriage than mere necessity. With the cold reality of what she had done, and what it would mean to her, she had to examine her motives. Last night, in spite of her anger with Adam for his arrogance and high-handedness, she had felt a keen sense of loss when she had quarreled with him. Today she had felt a sense of satisfaction and relief when she had told Sir Nigel of her marriage to Adam. Did she in her heart of hearts wish to be Adam's wife despite her belief that they were ill suited in so many ways? Was she, like her father had once been with her mother, in love with him, so that her sense held no sway with her sensibilities? Her common-sensical self deplored it, but her heart exulted and she knew it must be true.

Her most immediate difficulty was facing Adam. She now both longed for this meeting and dreaded it. How could she face him so soon after telling him that nothing would induce her to be his wife. Even if she did not admit that she had been forced to her decision, would he not wonder at it? It smacked of cream-pot love and she did not see how she could, in good conscience, be other than honest with him. She would go to him now as his wife, if he still wished to have her, but she still feared for their future and believed that their incompatibility must eventually surface. If it were not to serve her convenience, she could not honestly say that she would have come around to admitting her feelings for him and accepting him as her husband.

She would be well served if he laughed in her face. He would not, of course. He would smile at her in that lazy way of his and bow to her capriciousness. His honor and pride would allow him no other course. There was no point in putting it off; she resolved to go to him at once.

When she went to her bedchamber to dress for the street, she sent for her maid and dealt with the girl summarily. She did not dismiss Betsy—though she would certainly speak with her mother about the new footman—but she made it clear that she considered her trust betrayed and that while she might remain with Miss Leonora, if she wished, Willa would no longer require her services as a personal servant and would at once seek to replace her. When Willa informed her that she was Lady Revis and that her loose tongue was forcing her to announce her marriage before she wished, the maid became so vaporish that there was no question at all of her coming with Willa to Adam's house on Albemarle Street.

So, despite its odd look, Willa set out to call upon Adam alone, a very improper thing for an unmarried woman to do. But, as she reflected during the short carriage ride to his house, she was no longer an unmarried woman and had better right than any to be alone with this man in his house, which would now be hers as well.

When the door was opened to her by his butler, she gave her maiden name and he did not betray in any way that her found anything odd in her visit. He left her in a small saloon while he went to see if his master was at home, and alone, anxiety began to creep up on her. What if he refused to see her? What if he chose to deny after all that their odd marriage was valid?

But in very short order he came to her himself. As he greeted her, she was aware that there was something different about him. There was nothing specific in the way that he looked; he was impeccably dressed in a blue coat of Bath cloth, buff pantaloons, and fashionable Hessian boots adorned with glistening silver tassels. He smiled when he took her hand, but she imagined it was without his usual warmth. Yet there seemed no special stiffness in his manner, only a bit of quite natural reserve.

"Is all well with you?" she said, not by way of a greeting but with a sudden concern.

He seemed a little surprised by her question. "In a general way, yes. I collect you note my want of luster; I assure you it is nothing that a few more hours of sobriety won't cure."

She was dismayed. "Are you foxed?"

"At half-past noon? My dear Willa, if you think that, I don't wonder that you dismiss me as a rattle. I am merely suffering the effects of a night spent in Cribb's Parlor with Wykneham, whose wife presented him with an heir while we were in Scotland. I won a pony on the outcome of her confinement, by the way."

Willa's dismay grew instead of lessened. She could not but deplore the tendency of gentlemen to bet on such indelicate matters as the sex of an unborn child, and she had not had the least idea that he was given to imbibing to the point of being castaway. It brought home to her all that she disapproved of in his character and once again she felt the fear for their future. It was on this pessimistic thought that she began. "I have come to speak to you about us, Adam."

"So I infer," he said easily. "You shouldn't have come here, you know. At this hour of the day you risk being seen coming or going."

"It doesn't matter. I have come to tell you that . . . that I shall after all be your wife, if you still wish it."

"I still wish it," he said, and then asked, "Why, Willa? It is so soon since you were so adamant against it. In fact, I planned to send word around to my solicitor to call on me today to begin the proceedings for the annulment."

"It is known that we were together in Scotland and traveled there alone," she blurted out, though until that moment she had not known that she meant to tell him the truth of her reason.

"How did that happen?" he asked levelly.

Willa told him briefly of Sir Nigel's visit to her. She still did not admit to him that Sir Nigel had ever wished more from her than a payment of the debts he held, but she said that he had been offended by the manner in which the debts had been settled. Consigning the truth to the devil, she implied that Mr. Sledge had handled the settlement in a high-handed way, putting up Sir Nigel's back.

"And what is that to the purpose?"

"Nothing," Willa replied. "Only, it happens that Sir Nigel also had hint of our journey and he is angry enough with me that I feared for his discretion. I told him that we were wed."

Her explanation sounded stupid to her in her own ears, but Adam did not ask her to elaborate. There was something in his manner—she could not say what—that made her think that he was not deceived by her omissions. But if he expected that there was more, he kept his suspicions to himself.

When he smiled, she detected only the smallest trace of irony. "And so you will have me after all. My dear, I am honored."

Color tinted her cheeks, though his reaction was not nearly so bad as she had expected. "I could not dissemble on a matter of such moment," she said stiffly.

"No, I know you could not. It is one of your charms, I assure you. I would rather this, you know, than cream-pot love. We shall deal together, Willa. *I* have always thought so."

"Then you still wish to have me as your wife?"

"I thought I had already said so."

Willa felt a sense of relief and entrapment at the same time. She was in no position to make demands of him now, she knew, but there was one condition she meant to impose on him. "There is one thing that I wish for in this," she said. "I wish us to be married again, but properly this time. I believe you that we are legally married, Adam, but I wish to have proper marriage lines. It would be best for our future and . . . and should there be any question of the succession." She looked away from him as she said this last, pulling her gloves nervously through her hands as she spoke.

She had refused his offer of a chair when he entered, and they stood near the center of the room as they spoke. "Would you mind very much if we sat?" he asked. "I cannot while you stand, and the aftereffects of Blue Ruin are decidedly unconducive to comfort on one's feet."

She felt too uncomfortable to be still, but she complied, placing herself on the edge of a straight-backed chair.

He cast himself into a more comfortable wing chair and slouched with a sigh. "That is very much better," he said, his voice a pronounced drawl. "Now we may get on with it. I quite agree to your wish, and there is the succession to consider, but if we are to have the tree with no bark on it today, I think we should understand each other in all respects. You do not really wish for this marriage, I know. It is then a marriage of convenience. If you cannot return my regard, you are hardly to be blamed, but if it is to be a marraige *à la mode*, it would be best, for my comfort if not for yours, if we maintained a sort of distance. I shall want an heir eventually, I suppose, but the idea of siring one out of duty leaves me with a faint distaste. One can only hope that in the future either you or I shall feel differently on the matter."

Willa was stunned. She had not spoken to him of the feelings that she thought she had for him, because they were too new to her and they frightened her, but she had supposed that their intimacy, now that they were married, would solve that dilemma for her. His rejection then of her person and, unbeknownst, her heart was a heavy blow. "I don't think I understand you," she said in a tight voice, though she thought she understood him very well.

"It is not my intention to be oblique," he said apologetically. "Until and unless we can come together in quite a different way, I wish for this to be a marriage in name alone."

Willa had never thought of suggesting that herself and she felt as if he had struck her. Like everyone else, she had certainly known an amount of rejection in her life, but it had never hurt like this before. She prayed that her expression did not show how stricken she felt. "Of course," she agreed, marveling at the steadiness of her voice. "It would doubtless be best that way."

There remained only the details to settle. Adam would procure a special license at once and arrange for a discreet clergyman to officiate. She suggested, and he agreed, that her mother only be told that they had decided after all to remain married, for Willa had no wish for tedious explanations.

Willa was only too glad to bring the discussion to an end. She rose with alacrity and he walked with her to the door while she pulled on her gloves. The tremor in her hands was less easy to control than the one in her voice, and she dropped one of her gloves just as they were quitting the room.

He bent to retrieve it, but when she went to take it from him, he held it firm in his grip. Their eyes met over the small piece of kid and he said softly, "I still want you, Willa; that hasn't changed. But I want you as my eager lover, with no doubts or conditions brought to our bed. It is my damnable pride that makes me so, I fear." He released his half of the glove.

Willa did not know what to say to this; so, after meeting his eyes for a long moment, she turned abruptly and left him. He did not follow her into the hall, and when she again sat in her carriage, she carried with her that last picture of him staring down at her, his expression suddenly inflexible.

When Lady Anne and Leonora returned later that day and Willa informed them of her change of heart, Lady Anne was nothing short of ecstatic and fully concurred with their plan to have a proper English wedding on the following day.

"For it is always best to be sure," she said. "This is above all things famous! You will see, my love, that you have made quite the right decision. My goodness, I never hoped for nearly so fine a match for you!"

Willa and Leonora exchanged smiling glances at this, and when Lady Anne retired to her room to discover which of her gowns would best suit her daughter's wedding, Leonora remained to hug her sister and genuinely wish her happy.

"I am so glad you have made this choice, Willa," she said. "I like Adam very much myself, and whether or not you care for such things, you must admit he is a splendid match."

Willa could not help a rueful laugh. "I have done well in the world whether I wished to or not."

Leonora was silent for a moment and then she said a bit defiantly, "I have seen Lord Seton several times in this past week and he has hinted very strongly to me that he intends to call on Mama to ask to pay his addresses as soon as our mourning has ended."

Willa's expression became concerned. "Is this the match you truly wish for?"

"Mama is in alt about it," Leonora replied evasively. "She says that he is exactly the sort of husband a young woman who wishes to cut a dash in the world should have to guide her. I *do* wish that, you know."

"Oh, Nora," Willa said, sighing heavily. "I fear you are right; if it were a perfect world, it would be you that Adam wished for his wife. I don't think he would suit you as well as Stephen in all respects except for worldly considerations, but at least he has sense and conversation and you would have the position you wish."

Leonora chose to ignore the slur against her newest suitor and said instead, "But then you should not have had him, silly." She went over to where her sister sat, and sitting on the arm of the chair, embraced her with a quick, comforting hug. "I know your marriage to Adam has come about under such odd conditions that you cannot like it, but, Willa, if you will just give him and yourself a chance, I know you will be happy in it. You are always saying that you think you know what would best suit me; allow me to think the same for you."

Willa looked up at her with a smile. "Does that mean you will refuse an offer from Seton and accept one from Stephen, as *I* have advised you?"

Leonora looked discomfited. "I don't know," she said honestly. "I do promise you this, though: I shall do my very best to *do* what is best."

Willa felt all the burden of not having done very well herself by the ideal she had preached to her sister, and she could not say more, but her heart was made heavy by the news that Leonora would consider marriage to a man who had nothing to recommend him but position and wealth. It added much to her mood, already inclined to be fatalistic.

Everything was accomplished on the next day exactly as Adam had outlined it for Willa. He arrived early the next morning with a clergyman in tow to perform the brief ceremony in Lady Anne's best drawing room. He was accompanied by his good friend Lord Hartley, who was clearly not completely in his confidence, to serve as his best man, and Leonora did the office of witness for her sister. Afterward they all sat down to an awkward quarter-hour over sherry and biscuits, and when all of Willa's baggage that was to go with her to Albemarle Street was ready, she kissed her mother and sister a somewhat breathless good-bye and allowed herself to be handed into the carriage that would take her away from the security of her maidenhood and family. She was a married woman now and nothing in her life would ever again be the same.

If Adam noticed her odd humor, he said nothing to indicate it. His conversation was light and largely inconsequential, never touching on the personal. When they reached the house, he tactfully had his housekeeper take Willa to her room and made no effort at all to be private with her.

Willa spent some time with the housekeeper, learning from her the ritual of the house, conferring with her on future plans, and requesting that one of the housemaids be temporarily elevated to wait on her until she could find a suitable dresser to replace Betsy. When the nervous young girl arrived at her rooms, she and Willa spent the remainder of the morning unpacking and getting acquainted. With her time taken up in such fashion, Willa did not again see Adam until she went downstairs for luncheon.

"I have been thinking, my love," he said, looking up from the book he had been reading when she tracked him down in the library, "that the announcement of our wedding should appear in the *Post* tomorrow. Since none but us and your mother and sister know the actual date of our marriage, we can begin to receive at once, if you wish, without it looking odd. But perhaps you might not care for that. If you would rather avoid the dowagers and the rattles until the wonder of it dies down, we could go to Kent for a month or so."

Though she had never seen it, she had heard that his home in Kent, Weatherly, was a showplace of the county. Not a grand palace, but exquisitely and elegantly proportioned in both house and grounds. This, too, would now be her home, and besides wishing to be away from the gossips of the *ton*, she was anxious to see it. But in spite of the ease they had enjoyed together in Scotland, she was a bit shy of him now, and the prospect of a month alone with him, under the awkward circumstances of their relationship, was somewhat daunting. "But it is the height of the Season," she said. "You will not like to leave London for an extended time now."

He laughed and the expression in his eyes was sardonic. "There is always Brighton," he said blandly. "I think we can contrive to miss a ball or two and a few assemblies at Almack's this one Season."

Willa knew he was quizzing her and smiled. "Yes, but what of Cribb's Parlor?"

"I'll take sufficient Blue Ruin with me to drink the health of my friends and I won't care where I am."

Willa laughed with him and it was just what was needed to end her stiffness. From that moment on, the awkwardness that might have marred their early days together dissipated. She did approve his plan to leave town for the month, and within the week they were journeying to Kent, leaving Lady Anne to deal with the wonder and the gossip, which she did with great relish, having married off her bookish daughter to such great advantage.

Weatherly was everything that Willa had heard, and she fell in love with the estate the moment she laid eyes upon it. She truly did not care for *things*, but she could not help a small sensation of pride of ownership when she realized that she would now be Weatherly's mistress. Like the house in Albemarle Street, Weatherly was elegantly and tastefully decorated, and though he offered her a free hand to change what she wished, there was little with which she was not content.

This time at Weatherly brought Willa more contentment than she would have dreamed possible in her unwished-for marriage. She and Adam got on perfectly with never so much as a sharp word to mar their harmony. As they had when visiting his Aunt Maria, they shared and enjoyed a very simple way of life. Touring the estate with him on long leisurely rides, she discovered that he was an excellent landlord, both liked and respected by his tenants; as conscientious in his duty toward them as he was in seeing that his land was profitable. In town she knew he had something of the reputation of a fashionable care-for-nobody, but no one who could see him managing his estates and dealing with his people would say so, she was certain.

Adam had sent the news of his marriage and their arrival before them to Kent, so by the time they arrived, the whole of the neighborhood was aware that Weatherly again had a mistress. But for the first fortnight, their neighbors were all tact and left them to their privacy. If they had wished it, they might have put word about that they were receiving at once, but they were content enough as they were and found sufficient amusement in each other to make the absence of other company no hardship.

Adam kept to his word. They had completely separate

apartments, though they were in the same wing and adjoined, as was the usual custom. He did not so much as kiss her in a brotherly way. If anything, there was less physical closeness between them than there had been before, as if the simplest contact might lead to more.

Willa told herself that, given her pessimism for their future, it *was* best that physical attraction be denied; their only hope for harmony, she thought, was to remain friends on an impersonal level. But the truth was she was piqued by his apparent disinterest. If his passion for her in Scotland had been real, if he had meant it when he had said how much he wanted her, she could not understand how his control could remain so unwavering with so much intimacy and opportunity for dalliance.

The truth was that she had never in her life felt more attracted to him. His smiles could increase her pulse, his simplest touch was intensely erotic. It was only her pride, and a fear of rejection, that made her do all in her power to keep her desire for him unknown.

At the end of their fortnight's grace, their neighbors descended on them in a flood. From the day the first callers arrived, they never again spent an evening alone. It was dinner with Sir John and Lady Brent, cards and an impromptu dance at Lady Totterden's, a rout at Mrs. Henning's.

"I promised you quiet and respite from the rigors of society, and instead you are cast into a social whirl," he said in a deprecatory way as they rattled home over country roads from dinner and cards at the home of yet another neighbor. "We shall have to reciprocate before we return, I fear."

"Of course we shall," Willa replied, startling him a bit with the readiness of her response. "A formal dinner, I think, with great pomp, for some of them will like that, and dancing afterward and cards for those who do not like the exercise." Though she did not realize it, there was something in her voice that recalled her mother. "Not a formal ball on such short notice," she continued to plan, "but we shall certainly have the band that Mrs. Henry told me of from Lower Hamling."

He stared at her profile for a few minutes, thoughtfully biting at his lower lip, and then said seriously, "Do you mind very much?"

"No. I abhor the vapidness of society in general, but I am scarcely a hermit. I have enjoyed myself very much and shall like entertaining at Weatherly."

"The company you find here is scarcely up to the standard that was found in your father's gatherings."

Willa was amused. "You once accused me of calling you shallow; now I think *you* are sayng that I am hopelessly high in the instep."

"Perhaps we both suffer from our own brands of pride."

"Perhaps we do," she agreed, laughing.

When they reached home, she left him at the door of his study to go up to bed, and for the first time since they had formally exchanged vows, he bent his head to hers and kissed her good night. It was a chaste kiss, but it made Willa feel warm inside, and when he then bid her a very casual good night, she felt chagrined and could scarcely believe that it could affect her so profoundly and him not at all.

But she did not allow herself to dwell upon it or make more of it than it was. She went directly to bed as soon as she had changed and washed. After a futile half-hour of trying to find a comfortable position, she at last gave it up and with a sigh tossed back the sheets and got out of bed.

It was a warm night, and she did not bother to find her dressing gown or slippers. Lighting a candle from the tinderbox, she lit a reading lamp and placed it on a small table near a large stuffed sofa that graced the space between two large, many-paned windows facing the park. She picked up a book she had been reading earlier in the day, hoping it would make her sleepy and ease her restlessness.

She had not been reading long when she heard a faint scratching at the door that connected her bedchamber to his dressing room. She felt a sudden, not unpleasant disquiet, but the voice with which she bade him enter was reassuringly calm to her ears.

He was only partially undressed. He had removed his coat, waistcoat, and cravat, and the formal slippers he had worn to the party were exchanged for a more comfortable pair of house slippers. Over his shirt and knee breeches he wore a brocade dressing gown that hung open. "I saw your light from under the door. You told me you were tired. Are you unwell?" he asked, coming over to her.

She smiled and shook her head. "Only wakeful." Even a week ago she might have felt constraint to be with him in such dishabille, but now she felt excitement, not embarrassment. The nightdress she wore was little more than a slip of silk that clung sensuously to her body as she sat curled in a corner of the sofa. She had seen the long look he had bestowed on her when he had entered, and had read it with fair accuracy. His eyes were on her face now, but she knew instinctively that he was as acutely aware of her near nakedness as she was herself.

Whatever his feelings truly were, they did not show in his voice. There was only the languid drawl to which she was accustomed. "You should have joined me in a glass of brandy, my love. It has a wonderfully settling influence."

Willa laughed a little nervously. "Yes, I recall the last time I did so when we visited your Aunt Maria." She was a little astonished at the boldness with which she reminded him of that memory.

"So do I," he said with a faint upturn of his lips. He

took the book from her fingers and placed it on the table next to the lamp, then he sat down beside her and gathered her into his arms without the least hint of objection from Willa.

His mouth was warm and tasted faintly of the brandy he had spoken of. His hands, as they caressed her, made her skin feel as if it had begun to glow. She felt an inner satisfaction that had nothing to do with the physical but nevertheless enhanced it. His desire for her had been stronger than his determination that she should come to him. Headier spirits than brandy to a woman who had supposed not much more than a month ago that she would pass her life as a spinster aunt.

Whether or not he had intended this when he came into her room, he made love to her now without restraint. "Be my wife, Willa," he said into her ear, his face buried in her hair.

"I am," she said on a breath, and he got up and led her to the bed, where she had left the sheets drawn back invitingly. The small sound she made when their bodies were at last pressed together beneath the sheets owed as much to triumph as it did to pleasure.

It would not be accurate to say that after that night Willa gave herself completely over to loving him and the devil fly away with the future, but it was a beginning for them and she knew it was good. Her worries over their incompatibilities of temperament did not precisely dissipate, but they found little room in her thoughts, taken over as these were by the delight of realizing that she had fallen in love with her husband.

The month they were to have stayed at Weatherly extend to another, with Lady Anne and Leonora to join them for the last week they would be in residence. From there they repaired to Brighton, where Adam had a house on the Marine Parade. Lady Anne had visited the house before in the company of her husband, but it was the first time that Willa or Leonora had seen more than the facade.

"Good heavens!" said Leonora as they stood in the vaulted front hall. "Won't anything but a palace do for you, Adam? How many houses do you have?"

He shrugged. "Not very many, little one. There is this house and the one in London; Weatherly; a smaller estate in Pembrokeshire and a house at Bath, though that is little more than a cottage."

"Which means," said his wife dryly, "that it has only twenty guest chambers and two withdrawing rooms."

As mistress of the house, Willa found herself cast into a storm of activity as they settled into the house for the summer season made popular by the Prince Regent. The house was permanently staffed, as was Weatherly, but Barrow, their London butler, and their personal servants were added to flesh out the staff for their stay.

Willa was well aware that she had married a rich man, but she had had no notion of the extent of his wealth until after their marriage. "How could I have been so foolish as to think you might connive for your aunt's fortune," she said in a private moment that night just before they went down for dinner. "It is a shocking blow to my self-regard. I have always considered myself quite clever, but you duped me with the greatest ease." It was indicative of her contentment that she could refer to the way that he had married her out of hand and quite without her permission, in so light a vein.

He smiled in response. "Someone once told me that the simplest and most credible lie is one that comes as close as possible to the truth. Aunt Maria *did* send me the letter I told you about, but frankly, she might have left her money to the Society of Sea Gull Observers for all I cared. Nearly everything that I told you was the truth."

"It was such a preposterous proposition, it is lowering to think that I fell in with it so readily."

"You were in an impossible situation. Any escape was bound to be attractive to you."

"And you took shocking advantage of my vulnerability," Willa said with mock indignation. "I don't believe you would have called Sir Nigel out as I thought you might," she added without thinking, quite forgetting that she had never told him of Sir Nigel's offer to install her as his mistress.

His brows went up. "Why would I wish to do that?"

Willa could have bitten her tongue off. "Well," she said evasively, "it was he who placed me in my 'impossible situation.' "

"Reprehensible!" he agreed, still speaking lightly. But she thought she could detect a note of seriousness in his tone. "But that is hardly a matter for settling with pistols at dawn." It was almost a question.

Willa knew that if she turned the subject, he likely would not press her further, but she also knew that he could be tenacious if he chose and might well make it his business to discover for himself the truth of the matter. He stood behind her dressing table waiting for her to add the last touches of jewelry and scent to her toilette. She met his eyes briefly in the looking glass. "It is nothing, really. In fact," she said candidly, deciding to dissemble according to his own advice, "I didn't mean to tell you at all. You won't like it much, I think, but I pray you won't feel your honor affected, for I should dislike it excessively if the matter was not allowed to drop completely."

"You have me all in a quake, my love," he said in mock horror.

As she looked up at him again, she met his eyes, hooded now, but with something in them that made her think that his languid good humor was not impenetrable; he could be a hard man if he chose. "It is really a very small thing," she said as lightly as she could. "Sir Nigel *implied* that the debts might be canceled if I were . . . compliant toward him."

"He *implied* an offer of marriage?"

She didn't really doubt that Adam understood her; he wished her to be absolutely clear. She could not help coloring slightly. "I don't believe it was marriage that he offered."

"I see," Adam said unemotionally, and after a moment added, smiling again, "I must be flattered, then, that you preferred the risk of compromise with me."

"I would prefer absolute compromise with you," she informed him handsomely.

"I am unmanned," he said, placing a hand over his heart.

"I hope not," she said, laughing, very glad that the difficult moment had been glossed over.

But there was seriousness in his voice when he spoke again. "Do you still think us ill matched?"

She stood and put her fingers over his mouth. "Don't speak of that." She kissed him lightly on the lips. "I have come to think that too much concern for the future only takes away from the joys of the present."

His eyes opened with surprise. "My dear," he said in a stunned voice, "I am *completely* undone." And then he kissed her, not at all lightly.

9

The Earl of Seton had yet to come up to scratch as Lady Anne had hoped, and with duties to his estates to occupy him, he did not at once journey to Brighton with the rest of the *ton*. But Mr. Gordon was much in attendance. Lady Anne was ill pleased at this turn of events, for now that their mourning was over, she had been expecting every day to see Seton waltz into her sitting room to ask for the hand of her younger daughter. Thus would her cup have been overfilled; both daughters married with great credit in the world, and each to a title. What more could a mother be expected to accomplish?

Stephen Gordon to her was a nuisance. In spite of the fact that she had instilled in Leonora the delights and importance of figuring well in the world, she knew that the girl had a partiality for the young man, and beyond the fact that he would not be a grand match and had no title or hope of succeeding to one, he was not ineligible. If he called on her formally to ask for Leonora's hand, she did not know what she would say to him. Like her elder sister, Leonora could be willful at times, and Lady Anne feared that if she refused his suit without good cause, it could be the very thing to push Leonora into his arms.

Accordingly she did what she could to discourage his

visits to the house on Marine Parade. She remonstrated with Willa for inviting him so often for dinner and every other entertainment at the house. "He is my friend, too, Mama," she told her mother firmly. "I will not snub him because you do not like him."

Lady Anne disliked being crossed even when she knew she was in the wrong of it. "Take care," she said pettishly. "You should consult the wishes of your husband. *He* may not care to have another man running tame in his house."

"It is no such thing, Mama," Willa said, laughing. "You know as well as I that Mr. Gordon has no eyes for me. In fact, you object because you feel I am pushing Stephen and Leonora together. You cannot have it both ways, Mama."

"I may know what you are about," Lady Anne said grandly, "but does Adam?"

Willa did not rise to the bait, for to her the very idea of Adam being jealous of Stephen or of any other man was ridiculous. She had eyes for no other man.

Had Willa been more in a thinking mood than her currently buoyant spirits inclined her to be, she would have said that no one can live in alt forever, for the vagaries of life simply do not permit it. She should have remembered her father telling her that there is little sense in love, but she did not—not any more than she remembered the fears she had had before she had given herself over to loving her husband.

Though Lord Seton was not among them, the cream of society soon filled Brighton to overflowing. There were entertainments and amusement to equal the height of the London Season with musicales, card parties, and balls, particularly those held at the Castle Inn and Old Ship on Fridays to divert the most jaded palate. Willa, who had never cared for the parties and gatherings, found that she enjoyed them quite well in the company of Adam, with

whom she went, at first just to please him and then because she took pleasure in the outings. She was a little
amazed at herself in this, but did not question her change
of attitude.

The most eagerly sought-after invitations were those to
musical evenings at the Pavilion, the Regent's renowned
summer palace. The Prince was a man who on the hottest
of summer days could not be persuaded to forgo a fire in
whatever room he might be present; concerned for his
health, he ordered windows almost never to be opened lest
a malignant air bring him to his couch. The atmosphere in
the Pavilion, then, as summer advanced and the Gallery
and other rooms crowded with the ever-swelling ranks of
the *ton*, was at best sultry and at worst unbearable, to the
point that one or two ladies of delicate constitution felt ill
and nearly swooned.

Willa did not regard herself as delicately made, but even
the assistance of her fan was insufficient on an evening in
late June as she sat in the Music Room at the north end of
the Gallery listening to the latest soprano to take Prinny's
fancy. The audience was not set out formally for this
performance, but cunningly scattered chairs and sofas gave
the appearance that all were present for pleasure rather
than duty.

Whatever a couple's private inclination, it was considered hopelessly *déclassé* for a husband and wife to spend
their evenings in each other's pockets, so while Adam sat
at one end of the room near to Lady Anne and a few of his
friends, Willa sat near to the back, as close to the looking-
glass doors as she could manage, hoping that she might
catch a draft from the somewhat cooler Chinese Gallery.
But not long after the performance began, her hopes were
dashed when the Regent signaled a lackey to shut them
tight to prevent any draft. So she and the others who

disliked the heat were made to suffer with the rest of the
company.

In very short order the room became so close that even
her light, muslin gown felt heavy and clinging and her
head was beginning to ache in small spots near her temples
and at the back of her neck. Though she loved music, it
was impossible to attend to the performance under these
conditions, and she let her attention wander around the
room until she caught the eye of Mr. Gordon. His expressive countenance made clear that he shared her discomfort
and they exchanged a rueful smile. Though he risked the
wrath of his royal host, he got up from his chair in the
middle of the room and came to lean beside Willa to
whisper, "Are you feeling that we shall all be discovered in
the morning, suffocated en masse?"

"Discovered in an hour, you mean."

"Put a hand to your head in a distressed way and sway a
little and we'll make our escape," he advised sotto voce.

Willa did not succumb to these dramatics, but she did
rise willingly and allowed him to lead her from the room,
oblivious to the frowns their behavior received.

"Oh, dear," Willa said with a relieved laugh when they
had passed into the relative comfort of the empty gallery.
"I fear we shall be cut from Prinny's list now. Social
outcasts, forever doomed to view the glitter of royalty
from afar."

"I think I would hold a celebration of my own to mark
the occasion," he retorted, but then added, "I should have
a care, though. Nora would not like it if we did give
Prinny offense."

Willa sighed. "She is young and these things still matter
to her."

They began to stroll the length of the Chinese gallery to
be out of earshot of the footmen who flanked the door of
the Music Room. The Gallery was separated into five

unequal divisions by means of open, iron trelliswork, and he led her into one of these and said earnestly, "Tell me true, Willa. Does Seton arrive in Brighton at the end of the week and is he going to offer for Nora?"

Willa liked Mr. Gordon very much, but his obsession for her sister was causing his conversation to be continually centered on that one subject. He was losing his innate lightness and easy spirits and Willa feared he did himself no good by his intensity. "I don't know, but it is likely," she said gently.

Stephen bowed his head to hide the emotions he could not keep from his expression. "Then I fear it may be hopeless. There are those who would not find my suit ineligible, but in worldly considerations, I am bested by Seton on every hand. Nora wishes us to be friends; I know that she likes me well enough, but as soon as she sees that I am near to a declaration, she puts me at arm's length and makes it impossible."

Willa felt midway between sympathy and exasperation. "It might be no bad thing to give Nora a little rein," she advised him. "You don't help your cause by pushing her. Be the friend that she wishes and see to it that she always enjoys your company. When Seton returns, let her see the contrast between you in an open way. It may well answer, for there are times when I am not even sure that she likes him very well."

There were footsteps approaching them in the gallery, and Willa glanced up, expecting to see a servant pass, but instead saw Sir Nigel Allerton coming toward them. She was a bit more startled than the occasion called for because it was the first time she had seen him since the morning she had told him of her marriage and thus sealed her fate. But that fate had proved so gloriously happy that it put her almost in charity with him, for she was not at all certain that without that push she would have had the sense to obey her feelings and go to Adam on her own.

"Sir Nigel," she greeted him pleasantly enough, "I had heard that you were in Dorset and not coming to Brighton this year. Mama will be delighted, for she has declared that all of her cronies have abandoned her this Season." Thus she distanced him as a friend of her mother's and not even a contemporary of her own.

Sir Nigel smiled a bit mordantly, but his tone was all amiability. "I have been busy on my estates and also visiting some friends. I read the announcement of your marriage in the *Post*," he dared to add. "I felicitate you, most sincerely."

Willa inclined her head regally. "The compliment from you *must* honor us," she said coolly.

"My dear Willa, you are always worthy of my steel," he said with a light laugh. "But please, let us sheath our swords. I would remain your friend, if you would have it."

This last was said in a tone of contrition, and partly because she was long over her fury with him and partly because she did not wish to continue her quarrel with Sir Nigel because of the comment it might cause, particularly from her husband, she smiled and said, "But of course we are friends and have been so since my nursery days." Which words brought another small, sardonic laugh from the baronet, and a wholehearted smile that even his detractors would have described as charming.

Stephen Gordon was not an obtuse man and was instantly aware that something of note was passing between these too. Given Allerton's reputation with women, he could guess its import. He was in no hurry to return to the furnacelike Music Room, but wishing to be of service to Willa, whom he did not think best pleased to see Sir Nigel, he nobly said, "I think that if we are not to be cast off by the royals, we had best go back and suffer with the others." He linked Willa's arm in his and would have led her away, but Sir Nigel stood in their path and made no move to give them passage.

"I have sometimes thought," Sir Nigel said quite conversationally, "that one of Prinny's cultural evenings ought to include a reading of Dante's *Inferno* so appropriate is the setting. I suppose it is blasting hot in the Music Room," he added with a sigh.

"Hopelessly," Willa assured him. "In fact, tonight was exactly the second time in my life that I felt as if I should faint. The first was when I was ten and fell out of an apple tree onto my head."

Sir Nigel laughed. "We cannot have that!" He moved to Willa's other side and gently touched her arm. "Go back, Gordon, if you can bear it. Lady Revis and I shall stroll in the Gallery until the rest are reprieved for supper."

Stephen's eyes narrowed and Willa could tell it was on his lips to remark that he, too, would then remain, but in this situation, with servants all about them eager to catch a hint of gossip, and in a mood to let bygones be bygones with Sir Nigel, she said coaxingly, "Yes, pray go without me, Stephen. You may say for me that you left me all but recumbent and then I shall be forgiven by Prinny, who does not at all like to be faced with a greater frailty than his own. I shall recover remarkably in time for supper."

He did not like it, but Stephen saw that it was really what she wished and had the grace not to argue with her or make any hint of a scene. Nodding somewhat stiffly to show his disapproval, he left Willa to the tender mercies of her onetime pursuer.

But there was nothing of the relentless libertine about Sir Nigel this night. He was the amusing and intriguing older man she had always liked. Any awkwardness or bitterness that might have existed between them was not allowed to surface, and in light of his amusing, inconsequential chatter, Willa found that the time with him actually passed quite pleasurably. It also passed quickly, and she was astonished when what seemed to her minutes later voices and noise coming into the gallery from the Music Room warned them that the ordeal of the other guests was over and it was time for them to join the others. Lady Anne was the first to come up to them to admonish her daughter for risking the Prince's offense, though she quickly gave over in her delight at beholding Sir Nigel. Adam strolled up to them in a leisurely way, and if he found anything to object to in finding his wife with Sir Nigel, he said nothing to that effect.

On the carriage drive home, Leonora remarked on a conversation she had had with Sir Nigel concerning the imminent return of Lord Seton, whom he numbered among his friends. It was apparent from what she said that Sir Nigel quite agreed with Lady Anne that Leonora should do all that she could to attach that fashionable young man to her.

When they were alone in the privacy of their dressing room, Adam commented to Willa in a passing way, "I don't know why Nora's future should be of any concern to Allerton, unless it is to win favor with Lady Anne. He certainly seems to have pressed for Seton's cause."

"I expect it is because he knows Seton rather well, but is scarcely acquainted with Stephen," Willa said unconcernedly.

"I was a bit surprised when Gordon came to me and told me he had left you with Allerton," Adam then remarked, still in a casual manner. "He seemed to think that I might wish to rescue you. Does he know that Allerton tried to give you a slip on the shoulder?"

His words startled Willa into dropping the earring she had just removed. He was sitting on the edge of a ladder-backed chair, removing his cravat. Willa turned to stare at him. "Of course not," she said after a moment. "But he is an astute young man. And in any case, I never said that Sir Nigel offered me carte blanche. I only inferred something of that nature from one or two things he said to me." She thought it best to maintain the half-truth.

"A semantic refinement, I think," he replied, and stooped to retrieve her earring. "I might have come to rescue you, but the program was nearly at an end and I didn't fancy a jealous scene."

Willa put the earring he gave her onto the dressing table, smiling a little as she bent. "Were you jealous?"

"No. I knew that if you had thought you could not handle Allerton, you would have returned with Gordon."

"I don't dislike Sir Nigel, you know," she said a little defensively. "He has such a droll wit and can be quite amusing at times."

"And at other times quite unlike," Adam said blandly.

"Well, in all the years I have known him, it *was* just that one time, and I do think he is sorry that he ever pressed me about the debts. He certainly wishes us to remain friends."

"Would you wish him for your friend?"

Willa shrugged and began to remove the rest of her jewelry. "He is Mama's friend, it would serve nothing to make difficulties."

Adam stood and shrugged himself out of his coat; it was commonplace for them to undress without attendants after a late evening and generally they did not repair to their own bedchambers but shared a single one. His voice, when he spoke, was still as commonplace as his actions. "I think, though, that it would be a poor idea to encourage Allerton."

"Do you think I mean to accept his offer now that I am a 'safely' married woman?" she said teasingly.

"I think that Allerton has proven himself devoid of honor in his dealings with you. You would be wise to have as little contact with him as possible."

Willa's lips parted in mild surprise. There was in his tone and words a hint of command. One of the things that helped to reconcile her to her marriage was that Adam was so very different from the husbands of most of her friends. He never treated her as his property or tried to control her behavior. He trusted her to behave as she ought and treated her as an equal, deserving neither correction nor guidance. But at these words she felt on her mettle.

"Since Mama is staying with us and he is a friend of hers, I can hardly avoid the man without taking her into my confidence about Papa's debts, and I do not wish to do that. And then, since we go about so much in the world these days, those that know of his relationship to my family would surely wonder if I were to cut him. You know what society is like."

"I have not forced you to go into society," he said with something like sharpness in his voice.

Willa was even more startled by this attack. "You know I do this for you."

"You needn't." There was no mistaking the edge in his voice now.

Somehow a simple discussion had descended into an argument, their first, and Willa was not at all sure how it had happened. She was sure, though, that it cast Adam in a new light to her, and she did not at all care for what she saw. He cast down the gauntlet and she gamely picked it up.

"Indeed?" she said silkily. "I think you mold your wishes to a desire to control me. I will have who I will for my friends, Adam. I admit that you have not been as high-handed as I might have thought you would be from the way you used me when we were married without my onsent, but I warn you, Adam, that if you try to take to rrogant tactics with me, I shall not have it."

He smiled at her in his lazy way, but his eyes were hard nd dangerous. "It would be a grave mistake to assume me omplacent. There is nothing extraordinary in my wishing ou not to become intimate with a man who would have nade you his mistress."

Willa felt her cheeks grow warm and felt an uncheckable vish to defend Sir Nigel, though she knew in her cooler elf that it was born more of defiance for her husband than iking for Sir Nigel. "He did not do so," she said warmly. 'You make entirely too much of this. His behavior toward ne tonight was all propriety and I enjoyed his company ery much."

For a moment he did not respond. Then he said levelly, 'I see. Then you wish for attention from that quarter?"

What could she say to that? She was backed into a corner. If she said yes, she gave him good cause to step in nd manage her behavior; if she said no, she was admitting hat she was arguing for the sake of argument. She cast lown the diamond pendant she had been holding in her land with angry force, and in the usual way of dramatic gestures, she was made to look ridiculous when she knocked over a bottle of scent and had to go scrambling after it to prevent it pouring on the rug.

She cast a quick glance at her husband and found that he infuriating man was actually smiling at her. This fanned her anger and her determination to figure triumphant in heir quarrel. "What I wish," she rejoined with as much lignity as she could gather, "is to choose my friends without interference, and if that includes receiving the attentions of one of whom *you* disapprove, the judgment in he matter should still be mine."

His smile was still in place, but his features were set. 'Be sure of your judgment, then, my love. I won't let you make scandal for me, you know. A slack rein is easily tightened if the need arises."

His words were a deliberate taunt. "I am not cattle that you have purchased," she said with great heat. "Or perhaps that is what you think I am. My price was twenty thousand pounds was it not?"

"Is that how you think of our marriage? A business transaction?"

"Wasn't it?"

He came over to her, stooping to pick up his crumbled cravat and coat, which he had thrown over the seat of a chair. His tall figure seemed to loom over her, and for a minute her anger was penetrated by the fear that she had gone too far. When he spoke, though, his voice had resumed a fashionable drawl. "Perhaps it was."

A quarter-hour later, for the first time since they had come together in love at Weatherly, Willa climbed into a cold and lonely bed, not even sure of the comfort of having stood her ground.

Fortunately this disharmony did not prove to be a permanent state of affairs between them. By the next morning, both seemed aware of the excesses of their quarrel and their studied politeness to each other gradually gave way to the usual ease they enjoyed.

But there was a difference. It was subtle, to be sure, but it was there. Adam was careful not to insist that she accompany him to entertainments they were invited to, and she, for her part, stayed at home a night or two, not so much because she especially wished to do so, but because she felt obliged to make her point.

When she was in company and Sir Nigel was also present, Adam never gave her any hint that he objected to her sitting with him or standing up with him for a dance. Willa had scant satisfaction from this, for she did not especially wish for Sir Nigel's company and it seemed to her that Adam was more attentive to many of the prettiest ladies since their quarrel. Adam was not a spiteful man, so she could only assume that he felt freer now to indulge himself, and she almost would have forgone her pride and agreed to keep Sir Nigel at a distance if she could have been spared the sight of her husband flirting with women such as the notorious Lady Oxford.

Yet, somehow, Sir Nigel was always nearby. At first this made her uncomfortable, but he *was* an amusing man who knew exactly how to make himself agreeable when he chose, and in a relatively short time, Willa began to enjoy his company quite for his own sake.

As impossible as it would have seemed only a few weeks earlier, they really were becoming friends. He was not in the nature of a confidant to her, but she felt an ease with him that made him easy to talk to and he was always there for her to pour out any trouble she might have of an impersonal nature.

As expected, Lord Seton had arrived in Brighton that Monday and his siege of Leonora was more determined than ever. Leonora, still uncertain of her own mind, managed to hold her eager, would-be lover at arm's length, but with her mother's constant support of his suit, it was no easy thing.

Stephen, finding himself increasingly shut out of Leonora's life through the skillful maneuvering of Lady Anne, and fearing that Leonora was slipping away from him, reacted by becoming more grim and demanding of Leonora, trying to force her to choose at once for either him or his rival.

Leonora, torn in so many ways, at times felt almost desperate. "Sometimes," she said to Willa one afternoon as they strolled down the Styne on their way to Donaldson's Circulating Library, "I am all but convinced I am in love with Stephen, and hang being a great lady, but when I am with Marcus Seton, he takes such pains to see to my every comfort and I can see how it would be quite delightful to live with my every wish granted and the cost never counted. I just don't know what I am to do."

"Doesn't Stephen try to please you?" Willa asked. "There is much more to giving pleasure than with the things that money can buy."

Leonora sighed. "Yes, I know, but . . . Well, of late it seems that whenever we are together he is forever being demanding or accusing and as likely as not we end in a quarrel. Sometimes I wish that all choice could be taken from me as it was from you, and I would just find myself pushed into the right thing without time to balk."

Willa demurred at agreeing with this, but she had to ask herself if it had really been so bad a thing. Their quarrel had served to remind her of the discrepancies between them, which she had been wont to forget, but she was still far from unhappy even though she, who had been so determined to marry with careful consideration, had found herself pushed willy-nilly into the match she had made.

Her advice to her sister, then, was not in line with the facts of her own case, but rather that she not allow either Mr. Gordon or Lord Seton and her mama to force her hand to a course she might later regret.

There was a special dinner and entertainment planned that night by the Prince Regent which was for gentlemen only. The ladies were invited to a more genteel entertainment, but Willa, who had fallen behind in her reading and correspondence in her sudden entrance into the social whirl, cried off to stay at home and catch up with both. After taking dinner from a tray alone in her sitting room, she curled into a comfortable chair and began with delighted anticipation a new offering by a favorite author.

When Barrow himself came to her a little later to inform

ier, in a voice so expressionless that it showed his disapproval, that a woman, heavily veiled and offering no card,
was wishful of an audience, she was surprised enough to
find her curiosity piqued.

She agreed to see her, and when Willa entered the
saloon, the woman rose instantly, almost impatiently. She
was incongruously dressed in a lavender silk evening gown
elaborately studded with seed pearls and a walking bonnet
so wrapped about in a dark veil that she might have been
in deep mourning. As soon as Barrow had shut the door
on them, she undid her headgear without speaking and
then said with a relieved sigh, "That is ever so much
better! I thought I should smother. May we sit, Lady
Revis? I have a matter of import to discuss with you and I
wish we might be comfortable."

"Of course," Willa said, doing so herself. She took a
moment or two to recognize the young woman that her
sister had irrepressibly pointed out to her on one occasion
as the cousin of her friend, Mrs. Petrie, whose name had
once been linked with Adam's. Willa was a little startled
that she should call on her in such a way at such a time,
and not best pleased, but her breeding and curiosity bid
her to hear the woman out.

Isobella Petrie was an attractive young widow, not much
older than Willa was herself. She was one of a great body
of people who were vaguely connected with members of
the *ton* and who existed forever on its fringes. One might
see these lesser lights of society at the largest social gatherings, but it was seldom that they were included when the
company was more exclusive.

Willa could not begin to imagine what this woman could
have to discuss with her, especially in a particular way.
She knew that Lady Anne would have dealt summarily
with this uninvited guest, but Willa was a bit amused by
the dramatics of the woman's appearance, and she sat back

comfortably and encouraged the widow to allow her story to unfold.

"I am not come here for my own purpose, my lady," Mrs. Petrie said with a nice show of diffidence. "I wish to do you a kindness, you know, though perhaps you will not look to thank me for it at first."

"But later I shall?" asked Willa with a faint smile. "Please tell me at once, Mrs. Petrie. You must guess my imagination is running quite wild."

Mrs. Petrie shook her head sadly. "Just so am I cursed with an excess of imagination. It has led to my present state, I fear. Yet is has been proven justified and it is time for the truth to be out. We have both been sadly deceived in One We Hold Dear."

Willa bit at her lip not to laugh at the absurdity of this dramatic period. She half-wondered if Mrs. Petrie owed her style to having once been on the boards. "And who is this wicked deceiver?" she asked with admirable gravity.

Mrs. Petrie's expression changed abruptly, as did her voice. Instead of a copy of Mrs. Siddons, there sat before Willa a young woman with lines about her eyes that rice powder could not quite conceal and there was a weariness in her voice that went to her soul. "I know you are smiling in your sleeve at me, Lady Revis, but what I am to say to you is the truth and it won't make you smile, I promise you. Your husband is playing you false, the same as he did to me and, I expect, to every other woman who has had the misfortune of loving him."

Willa's smile vanished as she had predicted. "I think you had better explain yourself, Mrs. Petrie," she said coldly.

"Do you think we might have a bit of sherry?" the widow asked tentatively. "It takes more courage than you would guess for me to come here to you like this. I fear I shall need bolstering if my spirits are not to fail me. Dutch courage, I know you will say, but truly, I think we shall deal better for it."

Wordlessly, Willa rose and rang for the refreshment. When it was brought to them, she poured a glass of the wine for her guest but refused to join her. She watched with mild shock while the other woman drank the wine with a rapidity that she knew would have choked her.

Willa must not have kept her disapproval completely from her expression, for Mrs. Petrie smiled in a self-deprecating way and said, "It is not easy to be a woman alone. I was scarcely out of the schoolroom when I was married to Petrie, and the truth of it is he drank and gamed away every penny we had. It was thought a grand match by my family at the time, though." She paused to give vent to a wistful sigh and then continued, "You disapprove of me now, but soon you will despise me. The truth is this: I was once in love with Adam. No, that is a lie; I am still in love with him, much good that it does me. I know you will think it absurd presumption, but I once hoped of finding myself in your position. I won't say that Adam ever asked me outright to be his wife, but you must know that when a woman loves and believes that she is loved in return, she dreams."

She poured a bit more of the wine for herself as she spoke and paused again to sip at this in a more decorous fashion. "He did not even have the courtesy to warn me of you. I had no notion that there was another until I read the announcement of your marriage in the *Morning Post*. And then, that very same day, I received this." She opened her beaded reticule and extracted a worn-looking piece of paper which she smoothed for a moment before handing it to Willa.

Willa took it with considerable trepidation. It read:

My dear Isobella,

I know you must see the announcement today of my marriage to Miss Drake. You know that I shall always think of you with pleasure and affection, but under the circumstances, I think it best that we bring our connection to a complete end. I hope you will not be offended by the token of my esteem which I enclose.

It was signed not intimately but with his title, which gave Willa a little heart. Whatever Mrs. Petrie's attractions, Adam's regard for her had clearly not gone beyond them. Yet Willa felt as if a hand had closed tightly about her heart and then released it again quickly. It was not easy to sit with complacence before a woman she knew for certain had been on terms of greatest intimacy with the man she loved. But on the other hand, as soon as Willa had become a definite part of his life, even before their marriage had been consummated, he had brought the liaison to an end. In good conscience, however hurtful it might be to her, she could not blame Adam for the *affaires* that had been a part of his life before she had had a claim upon him. She had never supposed that he had been a monk.

She handed the letter back to Mrs. Petrie. "I can see clearly why you would be upset, but you cannot expect me to feel the same."

Mrs. Petrie produced a square of fine linen from the reticule as she returned the paper there. The reticule was designed specifically to match her gown and the small piece of cloth was edged in fine lace. Both were expensive trifles and Willa could not help feeling a pang at the thought that Adam might have paid for them.

Mrs. Petrie dabbed at her eyes. "It is my sad duty to inform you, my lady," she said, taking up theatrical tones again, "that your husband is as prone to the weaknesses of the flesh as is any man. In spite of his letter and generosity, he *has* visited me again. The very first week you arrived in Brighton, he discovered through friends that I was already installed here, and that very Thursday, I believe it was, when he told you he was attending a card party with Sir Henry Mildmay, he was in fact most of that evening with me." Her words were punctuated with an occassional sniff and the handkerchief was much in play. "I know a stronger woman would not have received him again, but as I have said, I am his victim as well as you."

Listening to Mrs. Petrie, Willa felt cold inside, but a detached part of her could not find this story credible. "If you have him back again, why come to me? You must know that there is no question of divorce, if that is your motive." She then added, not caring at the cruelty of her words, "If he wished to marry you, he clearly might have done so before he ever offered for me."

Mrs. Petrie gave a short bitter laugh. "Oh, I know that well." Then she looked squarely at Willa, and Willa again thought that the affectations had fallen away. "I am not here because I wish to cause either of us this pain. You see, I wish to spare you the hurt I have known. Forewarned is forearmed. He is faithless to us both."

"I am not sure I understand you, Mrs. Petrie," Willa said evenly.

"Do you know where is is tonight?" she said sadly.

"Yes."

Mrs. Petrie waited, as if expecting Willa to be more forthcoming, and when she was not, she seemed a bit discomfited. She said, "You doubtless think him at the Pavilion, where so many of the gentlemen are gone tonight, but in fact when he left here tonight he went directly to Lady Coombes, the wife of Sir Reginald, toward whom he professes friendship."

"Indeed?"

"There is no doubt of it, I assure you. I shrink to confess how low I have stooped, but I fear that as a heartsore woman, I am not above spying on my lover. The hint was given to me about Lady Coomes by a friend, and since then I have taken to watching the comings and goings on Lisle Street, where her lodgings are situated. The carriage bearing his crest came down the street and stopped before her door a little before eight this evening."

Mrs. Petrie could not be faulted on the time. Adam had left about then and Lisle Street was a quick drive from the Marine Parade. Willa honestly did not know what to think. She was vaguely acquainted with Lady Coombes, for Adam had himself made them known to each other, introducing her as the wife of a good friend who was currently serving with Wellington in Spain. Willa recalled that she was an attractive woman, in appearance not unlike Mrs. Petrie—or herself, for that matter.

At least he is consistent in his taste, she thought bitterly, and realized that some part of her was beginning to believe what Mrs. Petrie was saying. There was no real way to prove the story. She could not imagine herself having the self-possession to ask Adam outright about these women—and even if she did, would he tell her the truth?

He did attend parties apart from her, it was a common custom, and since their argument after the musicale at the Pavilion, he had done so with greater frequency. A flicker of fear made her wonder if she had herself made it easy for Adam to carry on an illicit *affaire* with not one, but two other women. It could not be declared out of the question and she knew it. Sexual infidelity was rampant in their social class; it was a part of life in the *ton* which she deplored, but never so strongly as now.

Willa was attracted by no man but her husband, and it had never occurred to her that it might be otherwise with him. Now she cursed herself for her naïveté, and the picture her fertile imagination conjured for her of him loving Isobella Petrie and Catherine Coombes caused her to feel a pain she had never experienced before.

She had the ignoble desire to take out her hurt on Mrs. Petrie, a very convenient target, but her good heart would not allow it. Despite her lively, intelligent eyes and handsome exterior, Willa found something rather sad about Mrs. Petrie. In this world ruled by men, there were many women like her, reduced to living by their wits and bodies, and Willa thought that perhaps compassion was more in order, though it took an inward struggle for her to achieve it and stay her sharp tongue. Mrs. Petrie and women of her ilk were still just women, as vulnerable as Willa was herself to the attractions of a man who made love to them and promised false devotion.

Willa did not realize how long she had been silent with her thoughts until Mrs. Petrie cleared her throat in a pointed way. Willa hoped that her thoughts had not passed in her face, for whatever she might believe, she did not mean to show any disloyalty to her husband before this woman.

"Even if everything you say to me is true," Willa said in a tone that was a nice blend of disbelief and amusement, "why should you come to me with this? Revenge? If you are without a protector at the moment, I cannot think why you would wish to alienate one who by your own admission has always been most generous."

Mrs. Petrie's chin came up. "Perhaps you have the good fortune never to have had your heart wounded by a man, but believe me when I tell you that it is better to know like this than to be shocked into the discovery as I have been in my time. You may not think so, but I tell you true, the pain is less when there is pride to salvage."

Perhaps Mrs. Petrie was a consummate actress, but

Willa could not help believing her sincere. Sudden tears stung at Willa's eyes and her throat felt constricted. Willa thought weeping over one's troubles a weakness in the first place; she would not let this woman see how she was struck by her words. She rose and said with aristocratic coolness, "I suppose I must thank you for your concern, Mrs. Petrie. No doubt you mean well."

Her tone and action were clearly indicative of dismissal, but Mrs. Petrie rose with reluctance. "There is much more I could tell you," she said leadingly.

"Perhaps," Willa said with a frigid little smile, "but it would be more than I care to hear." She held out two fingers to the other woman, who was not impervious to the snub and flushed slightly.

Before leaving the room with the servant who had come to usher her out of the house, Mrs. Petrie turned and said, "I do wish you well, you know." And succeeded in touching Willa in spite of herself.

❦ 10 ❧

As soon as Mrs. Petrie had gone, the cool, imperious viscountess, granddaughter of an earl, cast herself into a chair and wept. This was quite a new experience for Willa, to whom the joys of love were new and who had never been stabbed by its pain. She reminded herself that she did not even know if the things she had heard were true, but still she wept. Not even when she had faced the ruin of her father's debts and life had seemed impossibly black, had she felt so vulnerable and alone. It was not only her pride, but her heart that was trampled upon.

When she finally had command of her emotions, she returned to her room. She decided that when Adam returned she would quiz him about his behavior in a general way and try to judge by his expression and the tone of his voice if she had any reason to be suspicious of him. Unfortunately for her tattered sensibilities, she had rather a long wait.

It was well after midnight when Adam returned, and Willa had alternately convicted and cleared him of his alleged crimes so many times that she was on edge not only from the wait, but the mental frustration.

She was in bed when she heard him come into the dressing room, but she was far from asleep. She quickly got out of bed and slipped on her dressing gown. She went into the dressing room and he was just turning from the bellpull when she entered. He seemed mildly surprised to see her, but his smile was welcoming. He crossed the room to take her in his arms, kissing her lightly.

"I knew you would be at home tonight," he said, "but I didn't think to find you awake."

"I was reading," she lied

"I didn't see a light under the door."

"I had just put it out." She extricated herself from his embrace without deliberation. "How was your card party? Have you gamed away your fortune?"

Adam smiled. "The truth is, it wasn't a very interesting party, but I went because Hartley was keen on it."

Quite without a plan, her intentions unfolding before her, Willa began, "I had a visitor this evening."

"An amusing one, I hope," he said, smiling. "Or did you dislike having your reading interrupted?" His valet entered the room, but Adam sent him away again. He sat down beside Willa on a lounge in the corner of the room.

"It was Mr. Gordon," she lied again. It was reasonably safe to do so, for Stephen was not an intimate of Sir Henry Mildmay and certainly had not been invited to his card party. "He was at the Jerseys' rout, and after watching Seton pay court to Nora for a time, he came here for me to commiserate with him."

Adam sighed. "He is becoming a bit tiresome, I fear."

"I only wish I could help him more," Willa said, and then added casually, "He mentioned that he saw you on his way here tonight. I thought it curious, since his lodgings are in quite another direction from Sir Henry's house. He told me it was in Lisle Street that he saw you, getting down from your carriage and going into a house there. Lord Hartley doesn't live in Lisle Street, does he?"

"No, he has lodgings on the Styne." She thought she

heard wariness in his voice. "I had a note from a friend tonight who asked me to call on my way to Sir Henry's."

"That was very good of you," she remarked. "Is it someone you know well? I can't recall any of our acquaintance who live in that street."

He gave her a faint smile. "My dear, do I know everyone that you regard as a friend?"

"Probably not," she agreed, astonished at the easy way she looked up at him and the lightness she was able to bring to her voice. "But who is this friend, Adam? You are being quite mysterious, you know, and I am becoming suspicious."

"Are you?" he asked so easily that she could not believe he suspected any trap. "You need not be. You have not met Reginald Coombes, I believe."

"I think you told me he is with Wellington in Spain. Is he here? Has he been sent with dispatches for the Prince?"

He took one of her hands in his, gently tracing the lines in her palm. "No. He is still in Spain and in fine health, I hope. It was Catherine, his wife, who asked me to come to her. Reginald asked me to look after one or two matters of business for her while he is away and there was some difficulty that needed seeing to at once."

"Poor Lady Coombes," Willa said in all innocence. "I gather she has no family?"

"Of course she has," he said, looking up at her in a way she thought searching. "This is nothing to do with family matters. I could give you the details if you wish, but it only concerns some investments and is vastly boring, I assure you."

Willa almost decided to insist upon it just to test the extent of his resourcefulness. The truth was, she did not believe him. It was all too pat for it to be mere coincidence. She forced herself to smile again. "You would think me a jealous wife if I did." She started to rise, but he pulled her back.

"You need never be," he said softly, a little huskiness coming into his voice. He would have embraced her, but she moved back from him. "I—I am very tired, Adam. I think I could sleep now." She rose quickly and left him thinking she could not guess what. At that moment she did not care. If he did think her suspicious, he made no effort to come to her with reassurance or comfort.

The best lie is that closest to the truth, he had told her, and she believed it was exactly that maxim he had followed. Only when pressed had he admitted that he had not gone directly to Sir Henry's and he certainly would not have given her Lady Coombes name if she had not insisted upon it. If he was innocent, why not tell her all and at once? If he thought she was being too quizzing, why not say so? The answer seemed all too clear to Willa. He knew his conduct of the evening could not bear going into too deeply.

All at once she understood Mrs. Petrie. She had baited Adam because she had to know the truth as near as she could discover it. This was as close as she was ever likely to come unless Adam himself should confess his infidelity to her, which, knowing him, she could not imagine him doing.

Willa lay for a long time in the dark with her face buried into her pillow, though her tears were long spent. Having given her heart to Adam, she had done so like a green girl, so completely that her disillusionment must have been inevitable. No wonder her father had begged her not to think of marriage unless *all* aspects were considered apart from love and passion. Willa berated herself as every kind of fool. She had brought herself to this and now she was chained for the remainder of her life, unless he should decide to put *her* aside, to a man whose values she found

onexistent and whose style of life must be repugnant to
er. She wondered if he even saw wrong in what he did.
'robably not. His behavior was not at all extraordinary in
he world to which he belonged. She was the misfit who
onged for something finer, but she was not even sure
xisted. At this moment she wished she had sold all in-
tead of going to Adam with her problem which had
•rought her to this. That sort of poverty, she believed,
vould have been infinitely preferable to the poverty of
pirit she felt now.

As Willa dressed that morning to face a day that held no
•romise for her, she wondered what she was to do next.
)ne course was to do nothing. But she could not do
1othing when she felt so much. She did not know if she
1ad the courage to confront him, but she at least had to
•ut some distance between them, a padding of sorts to save
1er from further knocks.

She tracked him down late that afternoon in the library,
vhich he also used for a study. It was not a grandly
•roportioned room as was the library in the house on
\lbemarle Street or at Weatherly, but a saloon of sorts,
ined all about with cases filled with books, a serviceable
lesk at one end, and a number of comfortable leather
:hairs scattered about for reading or conversation.

"I have been thinking about us a great deal of late," she
:aid to him without preamble.

"Have you?" he said with no more obvious emotion than
nterest.

"I think we have been going too fast."

It took him a moment to respond. "Too fast for what?"

"For perspective," she said promptly. "The odd circum-
:stances of our marriage were such that we have been thrust
·ogether willy-nilly. I think a bit of distance would be a
;ood thing."

He was sitting at the desk writing a letter to his sister.

He put down the pen and cocked his head a little to on side as he regarded her with slightly narrowed eyes. " thought we have been dealing famously with each other Surely you will acquit me of self-delusion." He suppresse an exasperated sigh. He was heartily sick of hearing how ill suited she believed them to be when their relationshi must prove to her otherwise. He was beginning to thin that her ideals were pets to her and that she was simpl loath to give them up. "What is this nonsense, Willa?"

"I won't share you, Adam," she blurted out under hi steady gaze.

His brow knit. "Have I asked you to?"

Traitorous tears formed in her eyes and she ruthlessl brushed them away with the back of her hand. "You ma have your visits to Lisle Street, if that is what you prefer but you may not have me as well."

"Ah, I see," he said, and actually smiled. He was a littl surprised that he had not guessed. "I thought there wa something odd in your manner last night. But your suspi cions are groundless, you know. My visit to Kitty Coombe was as innocent as I told you it was, I assure you."

"Then why have you never mentioned your promise t assist her to me before? You would not have told m anything at all last night beyond that you went to Si Henry's if I had not forced it from you."

"Come, Willa," he said, holding out his hand to her in conciliatory way. "Enact me no tragedies. If you wish m word on it, you shall have it. I am not playing you fals with Catherine, upon my honor."

"You would say that, of course," she said scathingly.

He dropped his hand. "I don't know what more I ca say to convince you. I should have thought my word equa to the passing remark of an acquaintance of yours. I ha not supposed Mr. Gordon so officious."

"If it were only that!" she said, but did not elaborate. "

think we must do as we originally said. We are irrevocably
ed to each other and have come to exactly the end I
eared. In the future it will be the marriage of convenience
hat we first agreed to."

If she had wished to unleash his anger to gain her point,
he was successful, and it was no mean accomplishment,
or Adam was a very even-tempered man. "As you wish,
my dear," he said in a clipped way that bespoke a con-
rolled rage. He picked up his pen again and, dipping it in
he standish, began to write as if she had gone. Feeling
olish and aware of the anticlimax of the situation, Willa
athered her skirts in one hand, turned on her heel, but
he had not reached the door when he said, "You believed
rom the first that we would come to grief, but I never
uessed you were so intent on being right that you would
ontrive to bring us to it."

Willa turned and looked at him. She had never seen his
xpression so hard before. Even his dark eyes, which
lways seemed to hold at least the hint of a smile, regarded
er with a cold steadiness that was unnerving.

Before she could reply to his stinging words, he contin-
ed, "Since you believe yourself so conversant with my
ppetites, you will know that I am not a man to live
elibate."

She felt as if he had slapped her. His words went
hrough her like a knife, and it soothed her not at all to
now that she had brought them on. He was telling her
hat he now felt free to pursue his pleasure with impunity.
he would have died at that moment rather than let him
ee her pain. "And I am sure you will not object," she said
efiantly, "if I encourage my friends to call." She let him
nfer what he would from those words.

"If you believe that, my love," he said with a snap,
then you do not know me at all. This is not of *my*
hoosing and I shall not be so generous as you."

"Sanctioning my friends is not in your gift," she said i a tight voice, and casting open the door with some vic lence, she swept from the room in the grand manner.

But when she returned to her rooms, her anger an defiance left her to be quickly replaced by the misery tha had been her companion since last night. Once again sh elected to remain at home alone, for nothing in the worl could have induced her to put on a false smile and go ou into the world as if her heart were not at all breaking.

In the end, though, Willa was sorry that she had cor signed herself to an evening of solitude. With her thought so heavy, she could not concentrate on a book or even he needle and instead spent the night engaged in a great dea of fruitless conjecture over what might have been betwee her and Adam had either of them been other than the were.

She went up to bed fairly early, for she did not wish chance seeing Adam when he came in. Leonora and he mother were home early, though, and she was just slip ping into her nightdress when her sister, barely stoppin to knock, burst into the room and announced breathlessly "You are to wish me happy, Willa. In a month or so I sha be a married lady, too."

On the hand she proffered was a ruby of incredible size This alone should have told Willa the name of the happ man, but her own troubles made her obtuse. "Goodnes: Stephen must have mortgaged his estates to have gotte you such a betrothal ring!"

Leonora was accepting the happy congratulations of Wi la's new dresser, Miss Doakes, and it took her a moment t realize her sister's mistake. Her face clouded. "Marcu gave this to me," she said quietly.

"Oh," Willa said, and stupidly could not think of ar other thing to say.

Leonora said a word to dismiss the dresser and then sai

in a challenging way, "Aren't you happy for me, Willa? I know you like Stephen better than Lord Seton, but it is I who must live with my choice."

Willa forced a smile and said that with all her heart she only wanted her dear Nora to be happy. This brought a return of Leonora's smiles and bubbling enthusiasm. "Marcus proposed to me in an alcove in Mrs. Carteret's drawing room and it was quite exciting to be made love to so when there were people not a dozen yards away to know. Mama was in alt, of course. He insisted that we seek her permission at once, and as soon as she got up from a game of whist with Sir Nigel and the Pinkham sisters, he asked if he might have my hand in the prettiest way and of course Mama said yes at once. I think she would have told everyone in the room if I had not insisted that it be done with the usual announcement."

Willa tried to enter into her high spirits, but in her downcast humor it was impossible, especially since in her heart she believed that Leonora was making as big a mistake as she had herself. Leonora chattered on for several more minutes, but she could not but be affected by Willa's want of enthusiasm. "Come, Willa," she said coaxingly. "I am happy, be happy for me, too. Please?"

Biting back the choking sensation that came into her throat, Willa embraced her sister and said with all the sincerity she could muster that she hoped Leonora would be the happiest woman in the world as Lady Seton.

The next day dawned as bleak for Willa as had the one before, though the day itself was awash with sunlight. Lady Anne and Leonora had no conversation but Leonora's betrothal and wedding plans. Lady Anne began to make arrangements for a betrothal ball, thinking herself lucky that the house happened to have a ballroom, since many at the summer resort were not so formally equipped. Applied to, Adam, who had offered his felicitations warmly in contrast to Willa's reaction, agreed that Leonora must have a betrothal ball, and with all possible haste, before many of the first families left Brighton to spend some of the hottest part of the Season at their homes in the cooler countryside.

With his wife, Adam exchanged no words that were unnecessary and both were punctilious almost to a fault in their civility to each other. Finding the house oppressive and having been out of it so little in the past few days, Willa went out, ostensibly to change a book at Donaldson's, but instead she walked along the parade looking out to the sea, which she found soothing.

Brighton was not London, and it was not unheard of for a woman, especially at unfashionable hours, to walk unescorted, but neither was it so commonplace that it did not invite the direct stares of a passing young buck or two. Yet these seemed content or gentlemanly enough to only admire and thus caused her no alarm until footsteps that had approached behind her fell into step beside her. Willa turned, prepared to give a set-down, and was startled to see Sir Nigel smiling down at her. "Why so intense, fair one?" he asked in his caressing voice. "Shall I take you down to the bathing machines so that you can let the cool waves wash away the creases from your pretty brow?"

Willa smiled at his words but was not pleased that he had been able to read her so easily to know that she was troubled. "It has been a day of disappointments, I fear," was all that she admitted.

"And the day so young?" He linked her arm through his and placed his fingers over hers in a comforting manner.

Normally Willa might have rejected the intimacy, but she was not averse to a bit of comfort now whatever the source. "Nora has agreed to wed Seton," she said, deciding it was the safest of her troubles that she could share.

He nodded. "Lady Anne confided in me last night. You cannot like it?"

"I had hoped she would favor Mr. Gordon. He is so in love with her."

"Apparently his regard was not returned."

"Apparently," Willa agreed with a dispirited sigh.

They walked on in silence until the end of the parade and then turned to retrace their steps. Sir Nigel stopped before they had gone many steps, and his hand on hers made her stop as well. She looked up at him expectantly.

"Is it that that troubles you so, fair one?" he said gently. "Are you so distraught for the future of your sister or is it a matter closer to your own heart?"

They were not close enough for him to ask her such a question without it being an impertinence and deserving of a set-down, but before Willa could speak, to her dismay two large tears welled into her eyes and rolled silently onto her cheeks. He removed his handkerchief from his pocket and gently wiped them away.

Willa looked away from him. "I am sorry. I am in a brown study today. I think it would be best if I took my ill humor home."

"There is no problem that is not the better for sharing," he persisted, but Willa could not be coaxed into betraying more of her feelings.

She gave him a watery smile and said, "Truly it is just a megrim."

His lips seemed to set, but he decided against teasing her further and, with a sympathetic murmur, simply offered to escort her home, which she willingly accepted. If he was offended by her refusal to confide in him, he kept his feelings to himself and deliberately lightened the tone of their conversation.

Willa was very aware of his kindness, and regretting that she had been a bit abrupt with him, she gave into a defiant humor that was a part of her mixed emotions and invited him in for refreshment when they reached the house. She could not help feeling a little relieved, though, when he politely refused, and she made no demur when, having entered the front hall with her, he took her hand in a courtly manner and raised it to his lips for a salute. To her surprise he turned her hand over and gently kissed the palm. Willa could not snatch her hand away and create a scene in front of the servant who had opened the door for them.

It was just bad fortune that Adam, dressed for the street, should have chosen just that moment to enter the hall. There was nothing to show in his face that he had witnessed the small intimacy or objected to Sir Nigel's presence in his house, and he greeted the older man with perfect civility. The two men quit the house together, and Willa rushed into the nearest room facing the parade to see if there would be words between them on the doorstep, but each headed in a different direction, and if anything had been exchanged, it had been of the briefest nature.

⟲11⟳

In the days that followed, Adam was often from home. Sometimes they attended gatherings together, but even then she would scarcely see him from the time she alighted from their carriage until she was assisted back into it at the end of the evening. It was as well, for one time when she had been aware of him at the Pavilion, he had been in conversation for quite a full half-hour with Lady Coombes.

Lady Pamela Cuthbert, a staunch friend of her father's, called one day and suggested that it would be pleasant to meet again with the people who had comprised the main company at her father's famed Tuesday-morning gatherings. Willa, who often felt the dearth of stimulating conversation, agreed, offering her own home as a meeting place for now and Revis House in London when they were returned there.

But when they did meet, she found the evening no more than diverting. The sparkle that her father's genius had lent to the company could not be compensated for in her eyes.

Partly out of kindness and partly out of a genuine like of his company, Willa invited Mr. Gordon to the gathering. At first he refused when he met with her next, saying that he had no wish to cast himself before Leonora's notice now

173

that she had made her choice, but Willa persuaded him that it was nothing of the sort.

In her own heartsore state, Willa felt very bad for him. He was making a valiant effort not to wear his heart on his sleeve, but there were times when it showed all too plainly in his eyes. "You need not fear a meeting," she assured him. "Leonora thinks us a prosy bunch and has informed me that she will be spending the evening with her friend Miss Needenham."

"I wonder she does not call upon her betrothed to amuse her," he asked, unable to keep the sardonicism out of his voice. "If he can."

Willa gently touched his arm. "They are not wed yet," she said. "Perhaps I am wrong to give you hope, but I have noticed that since the excitement of being fussed over has died away, Leonora does not seem to me to be so content in her choice. There is a wistfulness about her. She is not in love with him, of that I am certain."

The look of hope that came into Mr. Gordon's eyes so affected Willa that she almost wished she had not tried to foster it. After all, whatever she might believe to be true of Leonora's feelings, it did not follow that her sister would cry off from her engagement.

Mr. Gordon smiled suddenly. "Do you know that she has sent me a card for her ball on Friday next? I could not decide whether she insulted me or was hopelessly naïve, but now perhaps I should regard it differently."

Willa had had no notion that Leonora would be foolish enough to invite Stephen Gordon to celebrate the success of the Earl of Seton. She could not believe that her mother knew of it and countenanced such folly. "No doubt Nora wishes you to know that she still regards you as her friend," Willa said hastily. "She will quite understand that you cannot accept it and likely does not expect it."

"I had not meant to come, of course," he said, his voice

meditative, "but after what you have told me . . . If she is not entirely happy . . ."

His voice trailed off as he pursued his own thoughts and Willa suppressed a groan that her well-meant words might precipitate an unfortunate situation should Mr. Gordon take it into his head to come after all. Thinking quickly, Willa said, "I think it might be best if you allowed Leonora to know her mind without bringing yourself to her notice. It is a maxim, is it not, that absence makes the heart grow fonder?"

Stephen looked a bit puzzled at her change of attitude. "It is also said, out of sight, out of mind. I think she must wish me to come, for it was her own hand on the envelope."

Short of flatly rescinding the invitation, Willa could only repeat that she thought it better to his cause to be absent, but she had no notion that he heeded her. He thanked her for brightening his day and assured her that she could count on him for Tuesday before going on with a decidedly jauntier step.

Willa sighed and berated herself for her total want of talent in fostering romance. The example of her own life taught her all that was needed to convince her of it. This well-intentioned but unfortunate meddling in her sister's life would come to no better end, she feared.

Much of Willa's unproductive time was happily filled with the endless planning necessary for the ball. When the night finally arrived, the fever pitch of activity gave away gradually to a calm that Willa unhappily likened to that before a storm.

The ballroom was festooned with roses and pink silk to make it seem a fairy-tale arbor; the extra help for the evening had arrived and was being instructed by Barrow; Cook had the grouse broiling for the more exclusive dinner before the ball; and even the musicians had arrived to set up for the evening. Willa, like her mother and sister, had had a dress made especially for the occasion. With Adam to willingly pay their bills, it was pointless to economize, but she could inspire in herself no enthusiasm for looking her best. Her dispirited humor continued unabated.

For as much as she had seen of Adam these days, she would not have been surprised if he was not to be in attendance at his own party. Not, of course, that she dressed to please him, but it was a symptom of the complete disintegration of their marriage that she felt the lack of his appreciation and recognized her need for it.

Leonora, from the day that she had announced her betrothal, had been in spirits that had at times seemed to Willa to be frenetic. But as the day of the betrothal ball approached, Leonora frequently became distracted and was often irritable, particularly toward her puzzled betrothed. It was Willa's opinion that Leonora was beginning to realize her mistake and feel the bonds of it. But one or two attempts to persuade Leonora to confide in her was met with gentle rebuff and Willa could only suppose that Leonora did not trust her because she maintained her friendship with Stephen.

Sir Nigel was one of those invited to dinner. Shortly after he arrived, he took her a little aside, and taking both of her hands in his, he looked her over, not with impertinence, but with flattering admiration, which gave her flagging spirits a boost. For the first time she felt that the fashionably cut gown of green shot silk made her appear to advantage. He also took the time to remind her of an engagement they had for the following day to take tea with an aunt of his near Cuckfield who had been a great admirer of her father's work. With so much to distract her in the preparations of the ball, Willa had forgotten it, but she had been touched by his description of the old woman's admiration for the poet and her great desire to meet his daughter, and she readily agreed to the time he mentioned for calling on her in his carriage.

Willa and Sir Nigel were not seated together at dinner but a little apart on opposite sides of the table, for her mother was acting as hostess on this occasion. They did not exchange conversation, but once or twice Willa exchanged telling glances with him when some point in the conversation particularly struck her.

Near the end of the meal, just before the ladies retired, she noticed her husband's eyes upon her. She met his gaze, not defiant or challenging, but letting him know that she knew he was aware of her intimacy with Sir Nigel and that she did not give a fig for his opinion of it.

When the ball began, she was formally led into the dance by Lord Seton's uncle, but all her other dances were flatteringly bespoken, and daringly, she had promised both waltzes to Sir Nigel, letting Adam think of that whatever he would.

Willa had been aware earlier in the day of a slight feeling of oppression that had made her make the remark about the storm, but as the night progressed most smoothly and the guests, which included Prinny himself, abandoned themselves to the revels, she relaxed.

To her dismay, Stephen Gordon did arrive late in the evening about an hour or so before supper. He appeared to be in good spirits, and after speaking briefly with a somewhat startled Lady Anne, he made himself part of the company without fuss.

"Stephen is here," Leonora said to her sister as the set was forming for the last dance before supper.

"I suppose he wishes to show the world that he does not wear his heart on his sleeve. I don't think it was really kind of you to invite him, Nora."

"He did not have to come," Leonora replied with a trace

of petulance. "And for all the notice he has taken of me or Marcus since he arrived, he might not have come at all."

"You can hardly expect him to wax enthusiastic," Willa told her tartly, and allowed Lord Cameron to lead her into the dance.

As the couples began to make their way into the supper room afterward, Sir Nigel came up to Willa. "Shall we go in together?" he said, proffering his arm. Willa meant to refuse his offer, for in spite of enjoying his company and wishing to defy Adam, it really would not do to set tongues wagging about the attentions he paid her. But even as the words of refusal formed on her lips, she saw Adam take the arm of Lady Coombes, who had unaccountably been invited, and smiling brightly, she accepted Sir Nigel's offer.

They did not sit at the same table as Adam and Lady Coombes, but unfortunately, they were across from each other. Willa tried rather pointedly to ignore the way that Adam bent his head to catch Lady Coombes' words and the teasing way that she struck his arm with her fan, but she could not help her glance from wandering in that direction.

Sir Nigel noted her distraction. As the room began to clear to return to the dance, he deliberately held her back for a private word. "It is a pity that you must be so used, my dear Willa," he said with gentle concern. "It pains me to see you so undervalued."

With a sinking heart Willa supposed that he, too, had noticed the flirtatious interplay between her husband and the woman she was coming to think of as that hussy. That he would dare to bring her into their home to flaunt their liaison under her nose was outside of enough. Yet Willa would not let Sir Nigel see how she was hurt.

"My self-esteem is not so easily tattered," she said with

a laugh that was meant to declare her unconcern. "This is your dance, I think."

They reentered the ballroom and the musicians were just returning to the gallery. Before they could actually reach the middle of the floor, Willa felt a touch at her elbow and looked up to see Adam beside her. "I have come to claim you, my love," he said in his soft drawl. "The prerogative of the host."

"I am promised to Nigel," Willa said, coolly continuing forward as if to dismiss him. But his light touch tightened and to have gone on would have meant rudely pulling away from him in front of the company.

"I am sure Allerton will forgive you," he said, not looking at Sir Nigel but at her. There was just the hint of a challenge in his well-bred voice.

Fearing a scene, Willa capitulated. "Please excuse me, Nigel," she said, her eyes asking him to understand. He smiled down at her with reassurance and readily abdicated his position to Adam. "Was that really necessary?" she said angrily as Adam embraced her for the beginning of the dance.

"Was it necessary for you, dear wife, to make it so?"

"Is that supposed to be a riddle?"

"I think that when a half-blind great-aunt of mine comes up to me at supper and asks who that man is who has been so particular in his attentions to my wife, distasteful or not, I have little choice but to think of your reputation if you will not."

His voice was not angry like hers had been, but Willa saw no fault in what she had done and wondered how he dared to attack her after his behavior with Lady Coombes. "And what of Kitty Coombes?" she said acidly. "*I* am not half-blind, I assure you."

"Lady Coombes came at my urging, for she is inclined

to live retired when Reginald is away and he also asked me if I would see to it that she goes more into society."

"And what a remarkably good job you make of it!" she said sweetly. "Kitty must be *very* grateful."

He smiled quite deliberately to infuriate her. "I won't pretend to misunderstand you, but I take leave to tell you that your insinuation is unbecoming." He was silent for a minute or so as they whirled about in time to the music. "Yet I find myself compelled to add," he said at last, somewhat musingly, "that if you were correct in your assumption, you could have no quarrel with me. I told you I was not a monk."

Even if he did not admit to his connection with Lady Coombes, Willa believed that he was telling her that he had no conscience for his infidelities. "As your wife, that must be my fate in any case," she said nastily.

He laughed softly but mirthlessly. "Let us have plain speaking, Willa. If you have decided that you will have Allerton after all to spite me for imagined crimes or whatever reason you have conjured, you shall find your fears of being controlled realized. If you think I cannot keep you from him, you will discover your error rather quickly."

Willa felt herself grow cold as anger swept over her completely. She might taunt Adam with her friendship for Sir Nigel, but she had done nothing to deserve this loathsome insinuation. "How dare you speak so to me?" she said in a hissing whisper. She would have pulled away from him, but his grip on her tightened.

"Do you know," he said with an air of discovery, "there is more of your mother in you than I have been wont to think. You have quite an unexpected penchant for melodrama."

"That doubtless explains the attraction," she said, her tone sharp and snapping. "Your dear Isobella clearly studied under no less than a Mrs. Siddons. Does poor Kitty possess the trait as well? I am sure she must, for it is in keeping with your style." When she mentioned Mrs. Petrie's name, she saw a flicker of surprise come into his eyes, and she added with an unpleasant smile, "Do you see how pointless your lies are? You have no secrets from me, my lord."

"I admit you intrigue me," he said thoughtfully, "or at least the source of your information does. I admit quite readily to the fair Isobella, but we are long parted. I have heard the *on-dit* that she is not without consolation these days. Since you are so well informed, perhaps you have heard it as well?"

How could his simple admission of what she already knew to be true have such power to give her pain? "I do not waste my time in idle gossip," she said in a constricted way. "I only heed the truth when it is clear to me."

"Well, that is a matter of judgment, is it not? In case you are behind the news, I shall tell you. Allerton's name has been spoken with hers."

Willa understood him. He thought Sir Nigel the source of her information and wished to discredit him, but she did not believe it. Her rage was directed entirely at Adam, and all fault was his. His smile was sardonic and she knew that he was reading her thoughts with fair accuracy. Her fingers itched to slap him. The tightness of his grip had slackened as they moved in the steps of the dance, and with a lightning-abrupt movement, she wrenched herself free of him.

She had startled him, but he did not subject her or himself to the indignity of gathering her to him again forcefully. Instead, he stepped back slightly and they stood facing each other, a bit apart and quite in the center of the dance floor. The couples closest to them had noticed and had nearly stopped themselves, watching them with barely

hidden attentiveness to see the scene they expected to hav
played before them.

But Willa had nothing else to say. She was perilousl
close to tears and knew that her anger had already betraye
her into sensation enough. Calling upon all her reserves o
self-possession, she turned, her head held high with dig
nity, and walked off the floor, leaving Adam to stan
partnerless or follow her lead as he wished.

She could control her carriage and her expression, bu
her cheeks flamed. She knew well that by the time th
music stopped, her argument with her husband, even with
out the particulars being known, would be the *on-dit* of th
remainder of the night and likely be all over Brighton b
the morning.

Forcing herself to smile, she walked around the perime
ter of the room till she came to the first open doorway tha
would offer her escape. It was an anteroom set out wit
champagne punch and lemonade, but as it was so soo
after supper, it was quite empty. Thankful, she collapse
into one of the chairs near the wall. It was a struggle o
several minutes before she could bring her emotions int
check.

When the music ended, she expected her solitude to en
and got up to go back into the ballroom, for she was in n
fit state for conversation with any friend of hers wh
might come into the room. She reached the door just as Si
Nigel was about to enter the room.

She started to excuse herself to him, but he took one o
her hands in his and said feelingly, "I saw."

Willa sighed unhappily. "Who did not?" She allowe
him to lead her back into the room.

"Do not tease yourself overmuch about it," he advise
kindly. "It will make a bit of talk, certainly, but quarrel
between husband and wife are scarcely unheard of."

"But they are generally not enacted in the middle of a ballroom," she reminded him dryly.

"I am sure the provocation was ample. I should not have allowed him to cut me out for this dance. My insisting would have made much less noise than this."

Willa moaned softly. "I wish you will not keep reminding me. It only wants Stephen Gordon to do something tiresomely Byronic like spend the night leaning against the wall staring smolderingly at Nora and Seton."

"I cannot say what Gordon is doing, but Seton has been in the card room most of the night playing whist for guinea points. I saw Alvanley just now and he said that the boy was pretty badly dipped. He called it a bad omen, but I think he was just jesting; he hasn't much opinion of the felicity of the married estate."

"A sentiment we share," Willa said bitterly without need of her audience.

"So soon, my dear? Or perhaps it is just the heat of anger?"

In her present humor and having already exposed herself, it seemed senseless to dissemble. "I have always thought it would be an estate for which I would have small taste."

"And Revis has not been able to convince you otherwise? I almost forgive him then for succeeding in your affections where I so signally failed. Do you know that in his salad days among his cronies he was known as the Conqueror for all the hearts he captured? What a comedown this is for him!"

Willa was furious with Adam, but seeing another, especially Sir Nigel, who was in some way a rival to her husband, gloat over his discomfiture, instantly awakened her loyalty. "It is the restriction and inherent difficulties of the *estate* of marriage that I cannot like," she said with a marked coolness in her voice. "There is no other man but Adam that I would have had for my husband."

"You should tell him so. It will comfort him, I am
sure," said Sir Nigel, unperturbed by her set-down. Sev
eral people had drifted into the room by now and one o
these, a Miss Valanet with a young gentleman in tow
came over to speak with Willa. After an exchange or two
Sir Nigel excused himself, mentioning that he would doubt
less see Willa on the morrow, and left. Willa was glad tha
the diversion had come to end that conversation, and much
of her composure regained, she returned to the ballroom.

But there was to be no peace for Willa this night. Whe
she entered the ballroom, nearly the first sight to greet he
was that of Leonora and Stephen seated on a confidentia
in a private corner, apparently in earnest conversation
oblivious of the stares they were collecting. Even whil
Willa watched them, Leonora was forced to turn her hea
away from Stephen as she began to cry.

Willa stared at them, aghast at their indiscretion. If sh
and Adam had not given the gossipmongers enough gris
for their mills on the morrow, this would ensure that sh
and her family would be notorious for the next fortnight a
least.

She began moving toward them, to bring the *tête-à-tê*
to an end as discreetly as she could, but between th
corner where they sat and where she stood watching, wa
the doorway to the principal card room. At that precis
moment Lord Seton walked through it into the ballroom.

It was evident to Willa at once that, in addition t
gaming, this evening he had been drinking heavily as well
His expression, seldom composed in a way to interest, wa
positively fatuous. He did not stagger as he walked, but h
moved in that careful way that a castaway man might t
assure himself and others that he was not in the conditio
he was in.

Willa instinctively looked about the room for Adam t
intercept him, but by the time she had caught his eye an

apprised him of the situation with a telling glance, the young earl had started toward the confidential. Willa moved as quickly as she could, but was not quick enough. Lord Seton reached Leonora before her and made the seated couple a lopsided bow. There was then a brief exchange of words between him and his betrothed. Leonora and Stephen rose together and the trio faced one another. Willa did not reach them in time to hear what the earl said to her sister, but Leonora's cheeks flamed hotly.

"You shall not say so," Leonora said to him, unfortunately raising her voice.

"But I do, m'dear," rejoined the earl in a sneering voice.

Adam had come over to them as well, but neither he nor Willa could prevent the disaster about to fall. Before anyone could do anything to prevent her, Leonora boxed Lord Seton's ears. A faint hush of anticipation fell over the immediate company.

Lord Seton did not respond, but put a hand up to the place on his face where the imprint of Leonora's fingers still showed. Adam came up behind him and laid a hand on his elbow to steer him away from the scene. Willa stood stock-still for a moment and then unhappily realized that her sister was wrenching from her finger the ruby she had once so proudly displayed.

Casting the gem at her intended's unsteady feet, she said, her voice choked with emotion, "You have the sensibility of a block of wood, and about as much sense as well. I wouldn't marry you if you were a duke with forty thousand a year." With this she could no longer contain her feelings and burst into hearty sobs totally mindless of her surroundings.

Mr. Gordon, who had also been a stunned spectator to this ugly little scene, reached out to comfort her, but Adam, not releasing his hold on the astonished earl, placed his other hand in a restraining way on Stephen's arm and

Willa quickly came forward to wrap her weeping sister in her arms and lead her from the ballroom.

What remained of the evening did not improve for Willa. Leonora wept incessantly and rambled nearly incoherently about how she had completely ruined her life and might as well retire to a nunnery since no one would now ever wish to marry her and the world as a whole was sure to shun her. Willa comforted her as best she could until their mother came to take over the task.

Even Lady Anne knew the hopelessness of glossing over the ignominy of this night, and was very glad of the excuse to retire and leave the seeing to of their guests to her daughter and son-in-law. Willa herself was hardly in a fit state to do this, but her breeding came to her rescue and somehow the remainder of the night was gotten through. By the time the last guest was shown into his carriage, Willa felt that if she had to smile one more false smile her face would surely crack.

When she and Adam were at last alone, they both stood looking into the empty ballroom in a thoughtful way. He turned his gaze on her. "An interesting evening," he said softly.

"What a talent you have for understatement," Willa said with a short, bitter laugh. Then she sighed and said, "Poor Nora."

"Rather poor Lord Seton," he said flatly, and then added, "Between you, you and Leonora have had a pretty night of it."

Willa supposed she should not have been surprised at this attack, but she was. "I might guess you would know nothing of another's suffering. I do beg your pardon for allowing my anger to betray me in public," she added with stiff apology, "but it was hardly unprovoked. Nor do I think that Nora deserves your censure."

"You may both run the gamut of your emotions whenever you please with my perfect good will," he said, "but I had the vain hope that you would have the breeding to do so in private."

Willa had no real wish to further her argument with Adam. Her fury having cooled, she was even beginning to be regretful that they were so estranged, but her overwrought sensibilities could take no more. "Damn you!" she said in a choked voice. "I wish *I* had boxed *your* ears. I think you delight in cruelty."

She stared at him and saw through the slits in his heavy lids that he was every bit as angry as she. "What I delight in, my dear wife, is propriety. You should study my example."

Willa actually raised her hand as if she meant to strike him, but he caught it by the wrist. She wrenched herself free from his touch. "You are as vain as you are insensitive," she said furiously.

He smiled coldly. "Such a pretty opinion you have of my character," he said, his voice becoming deliberately languid and unconcerned. "Constantly, I find myself enlightened by it. Perhaps I shall even improve. Shall I escort you to our—forgive me—*your* bedchamber, my love? No? Then I shall bid you good night, my wife."

~12~

Willa had supposed she had turmoil enough to keep her awake all night, but perhaps her senses were too overwhelmed by all that had happened. She fell almost at once into a deep, untroubled sleep.

The next morning she found that Lady Anne had taken to her bed, declaring in a mournful fashion that if she never rose from her indisposition, it would be a judgment on her unfeeling daughters, both of whom had disgraced her past bearing. She let forth an unrestrained wail when shortly after her breakfast tray was removed, she received a hand-delivered letter from the Earl of Seton stating that, given the circumstances, he considered that his offer for the hand of her daughter was revoked. She had had hopes that the quarrel could be made up, but now she believed her daughter's assertion that it was impossible.

Willa had looked in on Leonora first thing, but she had been sleeping, exhausted, no doubt, from the excess of her emotions. She was now in attendance on her mother, and despite her protests that it was best to let Nora be for a time, Lady Anne insisted on sending her to fetch her sister. She then called for her hartshorn to revive her from the shock of Seton's letter, and this arrived at about the same time as Leonora came into the room.

The young girl was dressed, her hair combed into its usual style, but there was nothing of the ethereal sprite about her today. Her eyes were swollen and there was a heaviness about her that bespoke her wretchedness.

Lady Anne, on seeing her, at once launched into a long tirade that ended with the words, "How could you be so lost to all propriety?"

Leonora sat in a chair near her mother's bed in dejected silence, all her usual spirit deserting her. "I am sorry, Mama," she said in a quiet way.

Lady Anne's anger seemed to leave her. "Well, if you are wretched," she said more moderately, "it is quite your own fault. I suppose that wretched Mr. Gordon had something to do with this. I always knew he had too much influence with you, and I shall not have it. If you are thinking, my girl, that by making this mess you will force my hand to permit him to address you now, you are fair and far out."

Leonora accepted the handkerchief Willa offered her, for her own, which she clutched in her hand, was soaked through. "After the way I have treated him I would be well served if he did not want me," she said, sniffing, "but if he does, I would take him, Mama, whatever you would say."

Lady Anne was shocked to hear such words from her usually biddable daughter. "And I say that until you are one-and-twenty, you will do as I tell you. From this moment on, that man is forbidden this house. And you," she said angrily, turning to Willa and quite forgetting that this was not her house to order, "shall not have him here under the pretense of being your friend."

Willa did not remind her of her impotence in this matter, for Leonora was weeping again and had unfortunately given herself the hiccups. Speaking quite curtly to her mother, Willa said that she would take Leonora back to her room to have her lie down again.

Though Leonora was not inclined to talk, she did try to explain to her sister that the cause of all this upset was that with the reality of her betrothal ball to face, she had realized that Willa had been right all along. Lord Seton might give her the position and wealth she craved, but she could not even much like the vapid young man, let alone care for him and wish to be the mother of his children.

"Well," said Willa consideringly, "it is a great pity that you realized your mistake so publicly, but I am only thankful that you did."

"It was only made worse when I saw Stephen last night," Leonora said, making a valiant effort to stem her tears. "He was all kindness and sensibility. I have been such a fool," she added, and the attempt at composure was lost.

It took Willa some minutes before she could restore Leonora to calm, and by the time she left her, her own head had begun to ache. It was upward of two o'clock when Willa, who was in her sitting room hemming petticoats with fine stitches to give herself occupation, was surprised to be told that she had a visitor. She took the card from the tray the footman held for her and saw the elegantly printed name of Sir Nigel Allerton. She had no more wish to see him than she did anyone else. "I left instructions that we are not receiving, Edward. Please inform Sir Nigel that I am not at home."

"I beg your pardon, my lady, but I did just that." He pointed to the delicate bit of pasteboard she held in her hand. "Sir Nigel was insistent, my lady, that I at least bring you his card and he wrote something on the back of it."

Willa turned the card over and read: "I hope you have not forgotten our engagement?"

Of course, she had. She had promised to visit his aunt for tea with him and his sister, Lady Meering, who was slightly known to her. She would not go now, of course, but it would be ill bred of her to send her excuses to him by means of a servant when he had gone to the trouble of calling for her.

She was dressed presentably enough in a morning dress of sprigged muslin, but her hair was merely tied on top of her head *en déshabillé*. Deciding that he would just have to take her as he found her, she descended the stairs to the saloon where he awaited her.

She was a little surprised to find him alone and supposed that they were to call for his sister on their way.

When she entered the room, he looked up from an examination of a miniature he had found on a table and smiled broadly. "How charming you look, but you are not dressed for our drive. Confess you did forget."

Willa gave him a rueful smile. "Yes, I did, but is it to be wondered at? Please forgive me, Nigel, and give my excuses if you will to your aunt and sister. Please say that I am most sorry and that I hope your aunt will do me the honor of inviting me again."

He did not acquiesce at once as she had expected. "My Aunt Jane is elderly, as I think I mentioned," he said, "and amusements matter very much to her. She will be desolate if you do not come today, I fear."

"You flatter me," Willa said, not pleased by his pressing her when he must know her circumstances. "I am sure she will be most content with the company of you and Lady Meering."

"My dear," he said with gentle reproof, "the whole purpose of the expedition is so that she might have the pleasure of meeting the daughter of her beloved poet. Without you there is no party at all."

Willa sighed. Sir Nigel certainly had the knack of successful persistence. "I would certainly oblige you if I could, but you were here last night, you must know that we are at sixes and sevens this morning with Mama taken to her bed and Nora constantly vaporish. I cannot leave them in this state."

"They are hardly alone in a house filled with servants, and then there is Revis, surely all should not be on your shoulders. If there is any further upset, he may deal with it himself. You deserve to get away from all this."

"You are kind," Willa said mechanically, "but Adam is from home today. He is gone to a cockfight in Horley, I believe; he mentioned it earlier in the week. It will doubtless be very late before he returns. Like it or not, it is left to me to remain to see to matters."

"Will you accuse me of impertinence if I say 'nonsense?' " he said with an ingratiating smile. "You have troubles enough of your own to occupy you and are needful of a bit of comfort and relief yourself. Come with me to my aunt for a few hours; it will divert you, I promise, and you will be refreshed to be able to deal better with any problems the rest of your family may have."

His argument was persuasive. She was feeling the burden of attending to the hysterics of her mother and sister when she herself could well use attention. "I had hoped that Nora might come with us, you know," she said tentatively, "but she is in no state for a drive or a visit today."

"You know that I always value the company of your sister, but it is you I am concerned with and it is you my aunt wishes to meet. My dear Willa, please come with me," he said, coaxing her. "I pledge my word that you shall find the diversion you need and very certainly you will save an old woman from severe disappointment."

Willa was torn. She did not really wish to go with Sir Nigel and had wished Leonora to be with her to make the visit look less particular, but the prospect of the bleak

fternoon that spread before her made her wish to get
way from the house. Impulsively, she agreed. "Very
vell, I shall come, but you must give me time to change.
Perhaps you should send a note around to your sister; she
vill wonder what is keeping us. There is paper and a pen
n the desk in the room across from here and you may ask
ne of our footmen to take it to her. I promise to be as
quick as I may."

Having made up her mind, she hastened from the room
nd Sir Nigel took her advice and crossed the hall to the
pposite room. He went at once to the desk she had
nentioned and found several sheets of elegant, hot-pressed
otepaper bearing Revis' crest. He also found a pen, a
nife to mend it, and sufficient ink to his purpose.

He tapped the pen against his teeth thoughtfully for a
noment, and then dipped the nib into the ink and wrote
apidly. He dried the ink with sand, folded the paper, and
earched to discover his last need: sealing wax and a seal.

Coming into the hall again, he noticed a footman about
o go through the service door and called to him. He gave
im the note, not with directions that it be taken to his
ister, but that it be given to no one but Lord Revis upon
is return. Smiling as the door swung shut behind the
iveried servant, Sir Nigel returned to the salon to await
Willa's return.

Willa did not disappoint him. In less time than he would
ave thought possible, she returned to him wearing a
Irab-colored driving dress meant to imitate the driving
oats that were the rage among gentlemen. She pulled on a
air of kid gloves, and a beaver hat sat jauntily upon her
lossy brown locks. She smiled at him with satisfaction for
er own efficiency and suggested that they leave at once.

He handed her into an elegant town carriage that he
nformed her belonged to his sister. Thus reassured that
he would not for long be closed alone with him, which

made her mildly uncomfortable, she relaxed against th comfort of the squabs.

But it seemed to her that they had traveled for som distance and she recognized that they were near to leavin the city. "Do we not have to fetch Lady Meering?" sh asked with a hint of suspicion in her voice.

"No. I fear that Margaret was indisposed today. Sh was kind enough to insist, though, that we use her carriage."

"You should have told me this before I agreed to come," Willa said uneasily. "It is really not the thing for me t drive out of the city with you alone."

"We are old friends, my dear," he said, sounding mildly surprised. "What objection can there be to so innocent a excursion?" He was sitting across from her at his ease, hi gloved hands resting easily on the head of his stick, which he balanced on the floor of the carriage. He did not hav the look about him of a man bent on dalliance.

Yet Willa could not like this. "It is not pleasant to recal the memory," she said slowly, "but your behavior towar me in the past has not always been in accord with honor. would as soon we were not so intimate as this visit mus make us. I wish you will tell your coachman to turn abou and we shall visit your aunt another day."

He sighed. "I had hoped by my exemplary behavio since that time to erase the memory from your mind. But my dear, what do you think I mean to do? Ravage you in swaying carriage bumping over a rutted road? Kidnap yo and take you to a gloomy castle on the coast? You read to much and grow fanciful, I fear. We must be a full third o the way to Cuckfield; it would be senseless to turn bac and it is certainly too late to send word to Aunt Jane not t expect us."

Willa did not like it overmuch, but again she allowe him to persuade her. Perhaps she was being fanciful, fo never since the day she had told him that she was Lad

Revis had he behaved toward her in any way that was not gentlemanly. Stifling her reluctance, she agreed that they should go on, and traveling for a longer space than she expected, they at last reached his aunt's house.

Willa had told Doakes to inform her mother of her whereabouts and had told her that she would not be back before dinnertime. She wondered how late it was now, and asked Sir Nigel for the time, for she had a sudden uncomfortable thought that in returning they might meet up with Adam, who in journeying to Horley would travel the same road.

She had used Sir Nigel to defy him yesterday, but she knew all at once that she did not wish him to know of her drive and visit with him today. In spite of Lady Coombes, she did not want to give him cause to think that she was playing the same game as he, and what might he not think of this afternoon's work, which, despite Sir Nigel's reassurances, definitely could not be called proper.

The afternoon with Sir Nigel's Aunt Jane passed pleasantly. Sir Nigel had greatly exaggerated, though, that lady's devotion to Sir Hammish's work, for when Willa gently quizzed her on the subject, Willa discovered she had no more than a cursory knowledge of her father's poems and was quite unfamiliar with most of his essays.

Tea was served rather late, to Willa's mind, and afterward Sir Nigel and his aunt insisted that they stay on for a while, first to walk in a nearby wood for the old woman's "digestion" and then to play a game of three-handed whist, for the old woman pleaded that she so seldom had company. Willa obliged in both because Sir Nigel insisted and she did not see how she could cavil without incivility, but eventually she became aware of the passage of time and knew they were detained long beyond what she had intended.

Sir Nigel fell into a somewhat involved conversation

with his aunt, which appeared to have something to do
with a mutual friend who had once been upon the stage,
and Willa, in her anxiety to be away, fairly danced in her
chair. In spite of several subtle and then increasingly broader
hints to him, it took her the better part of another hour
before she was able to bring him to the point of ordering
their carriage. That, too, seemed to take forever to come,
and Willa was tapping her foot with impatience, heedless
now as to how it must look. But at last the carriage
arrived, good-byes and thanks were said, and they were
finally in the carriage.

"There, we are off," he said to her as if to a child. "Are
you pleased now?"

Willa knew she was not behaving well, but was in no
humor to care. "I would be better pleased if we had been
on our way two hours ago at the least," she said waspishly.
"There is no hope now that I shall be back in time for
dinner as I said I would, and I can only hope we shall not
be benighted, which will slow our return even more. I
don't recall there is a moon tonight."

"About half, I think, but you needn't fear, Willa. We
shall be back to Brighton in good time."

But in her anxiety and annoyance, Willa could not be
cajoled into more than desultory conversation. Once again
the passage of time seemed to her to be considerable, and
though she supposed it must be her impatience, she was
becoming increasingly uncomfortable. Light was beginning to fade and the road, which was fairly smooth for
most of the drive, seemed to deteriorate. She supposed
that the carriage had turned onto a lesser road for a shorter
way, but before she could ask Sir Nigel about this, the
carriage slowed to a walk. Sir Nigel rapped his cane against
the roof of the carriage, and when they stopped, he got out
to confer with his coachman.

"One of the horses has gone lame," he said, getting in

gain. "Hitchly took this road to save a bit of time, but it
as proved the reverse, for the dumb creature stumbled in
 rut. He says that there is an inn not far from here where
e may be able to hire another horse, though it is not a
oaching inn."

There was nothing for Willa to do but try as best as she
ould to contain her rising anger and impatience. The inn
as soon reached and it did not seem to Willa to be a very
repossessing place. Most of the windows were shuttered
nd the place had a tumbledown look; the courtyard was
argely dirt, with only a broken cobble here and there to
estify to better days.

When they stopped in the courtyard, Sir Nigel again got
own and Willa assumed that he was attempting to pro-
ure a horse himself rather than leave the matter to his
oachman and groom, but after only a very few minutes,
e returned and, without getting in again himself, held out
is hand to Willa to help her down the steps.

"I would as leif wait in the carriage," she told him, in a
uzzle in any case why he should wish her to leave it. She
ertainly had no wish to go into the shabby inn.

"This may take a bit more time than I'd thought. There
s no horse here, but the ostler has a brother who lives
earby and he has a horse that has been trained to harness.
He is going at once to fetch it, but it will take a quarter-
our, at the least."

"If it is not a coaching inn, I see no point in waiting
nside in a common taproom," she said, not to be difficult,
ut because it seemed to her, somehow, that waiting in the
arriage would lessen the delay. "You go in if you like. I
refer to remain in the carriage."

He still held out his hand to her. "It would be best if
ou came in with me. There may be some sort of parlor
e can hire and we may have some wine and biscuits. We
re certainly missing our dinners, you know."

Willa sighed wearily. "How far are we from Brighton?"

"At least a half-hour away, maybe more. By the time the horse is hired and put to the carriage, it may be twice that before we can leave."

Her vexation gave way to resignation. It seemed there would be no end to their delays, and it was only feeding her frustration to fight against what she could not help. She allowed him to assist her from the carriage.

Adam did not remain as late in Horley as his wife had expected him to. Never much an advocate of cocking, he found the day's sport sadly flat and declined an offer from his friends to take dinner with them at the Chequers, the famed coaching inn with an excellent reputation for plain fare. Instead, as afternoon faded into evening, he called for his curricle and was soon on his way back to Brighton. If Sir Nigel's carriage had not turned off the main pike road some few miles before Brighton was reached, it is very likely that he would have passed his wife on her way home as she had feared.

Adam was a first-class whip, a member in good standing of the Four Horse Club and permitted to wear its much-coveted uniform, which made men like George Brummell wince and declare that being a famous whip was not worth the price. Adam had the ability to drive his team mechanically, using the reins and whip with such consummate skill that it required little thought. What occupied his mind were thoughts of the events of the previous night. He was distressed, of course, about Leonora, but it was only natural that he should dwell principally on the hard words that he and Willa had spoken to each other. He had never meant to let her see how upset he was by her encouraging of Allerton's attentions, and certainly he had not wanted to lose his temper.

He did not really believe that their relationship had gone

beyond a bit of dalliance, and he suspected that it was largely in defiance of him. She was determined to believe him unfaithful and wished to throw an admirer of her own in his teeth. He wished he might have had the leisure and composure to let it run its course, but after last night, it would not do. Willa's attraction to Allerton would have to be nipped in the bud, though it would doubtless harm his already disintegrating marriage nearly as much as if there were more between them.

Adam was both angered and pained by Willa's refusal to believe in him. Her information on his whereabouts and action had puzzled him until she had let Isobella Petrie's name drop last night. Allerton was no fool and likely had scented out the vulnerabilities of their marriage. Adam knew that he might be able to stop Allerton from dangling after Willa, but there was a harm done that might never be healed.

As he pulled up in front of the house on Marine Parade, he was surprised to see that every light in the house appeared to be on. He handed the ribbons to his groom and with a feeling of foreboding entered the house with Barrow himself holding the door.

Like any good butler, Barrow had been trained in impassivity, but there was that in his countenance which told Adam at once that something was amiss. "Don't spare me, Barrow," he said as he handed that man his hat and driving coat. "Cook drank all the sherry in the cellar and drowned herself in the soup?"

Cook, a complete abstainer who believed wine the brew of the devil, would likely have given notice for this sally, and generally it would have raised the hint of a smile from the butler, who liked a nip now and then himself. But today he remained unmoved, which Adam thought boded ill indeed. "Her ladyship wishes to see you at once in her bedchamber, my lord," he said awfully.

Adam looked at him sharply. "Is my wife unwell?"

"I beg your pardon, my lord, I should have been more specific. It is Lady Anne who wishes to see you."

"Dear me," said Adam obliquely, expecting that his mother-in-law was still indulging in the vapors from last night and intended to subject him to some of the histrionics he had thought to escape all day. He sighed resignedly "When I was at school," he said confidentially to his servant, "we called this bracing for your stripes. Is Lady Revis at home?"

"No, my lord."

Adam wondered that Willa would care to go out tonight and face down the gossips, and thought perhaps she had deemed it preferable to an evening spent with her mother and sister in their present state.

Seeing no point in putting it off, he went to his mother-in-law's apartments. When he entered her bedchamber the scene before him appeared to be in tableau. Lady Anne lay on her bed propped up on pillows with one hand raised to her brow as if in distress; Leonora sat beside her solicitously holding her other hand; and her dresser hovered discreetly at the foot of the bed awaiting her mistress's bidding.

"Oh, thank God," Leonora cried out as soon as she saw Adam. She turned and quickly dismissed the reluctant servant and Adam braced himself for what was to come next.

"Will my misery never end?" Lady Anne said weakly as he approached the bed. "I thought I would be blessed in my offspring, but instead I am cursed."

Adam ignored her completely and addressed Leonora "What is afoot, Nora? Where is Willa?"

Her lovely face was puffy from the copious tears she had shed since last night. "Oh, Adam, I wish there was some better way to tell you this, but I fear it is impossible." Her voice began to choke and she pulled a crumpled piece of paper out of a concealed pocket in her dress. Biting at her lip in an almost frightened way, she handed it to him, watching him read it for his reaction. There was no dramatic change in his coloring or expression, but the lines of his face became taut, giving his features a grim overcast.

Adam recognized the paper as his own at once, though the hand that directed it to him was not Willa's. He read it through once and then again. His eyes dwelt rather a long time on the signature, but at last he looked up and said in a clipped way, "This is addressed to me. How is it that you have it?"

There was a groan from the bed and the distraught older woman began to speak about the hopelessness of their ruin, but Leonora merely raised her voice above her mother's to be heard. "Willa did not return for dinner as she said she would, and when it became late enough for us to be alarmed, Mama questioned the servants. Edward, one of the footmen, admitted that a note had been left but insisted that it was for you. You know what Mama is, there was no peace until she had it."

Leonora took a deep breath and added, "I know you and Mama will not like it, but I have sent for Mr. Gordon. I did not think you would be back so soon and had the notion of sending him after you."

She had given the servants instructions to send Stephen up to her the moment he arrived, and as if on cue, he came into the room at that moment. At the sight of him, Leonora cast herself upon him and began to weep on his superfine-encased shoulder. Stephen appeared puzzled, but not ungratified, and applied himself at once to comforting his beloved and discovering what had upset her so.

Lady Anne sat up in bed and said accusingly to Adam "I hold this to be all your fault. A husband should have an eye open to this sort of thing and stop it before it begins Eloped! And with my own friend! I shall never live it down. We shall have to live retired for the whole of our lives, I know it."

Adam felt as if his head were spinning. He took a deep breath to steady himself, and then turned to his mother-in law and said as sharply as he had ever spoken to her, "You have made a pretty mess of this! You have a great concern for scandal but none at all for discretion."

"What difference does it make if the servants know now or later?" she responded acerbically. "You can't hush up a thing like this. There is nothing at all to be done about it."

"There is always something to be done, madam, and hysterics are not to the purpose."

Lady Anne sniffed indignantly and fell back on her pillows. Adam looked toward where Stephen had led Leonora to a couch. Her tears were dried and she smiled up at him as if she had found her savior. It seemed to him that both had given Willa up as lost to them and were looking only to their own comfort. It filled him with a sudden disgust. For a moment, he himself, after reading the calculated insults that Sir Nigel had written, had had the base thought to leave Willa to her fate if she preferred Allerton to him, but even if that were the truth, he could not do it.

Cutting in on the soft-spoken conversation of Leonora and Stephen, he demanded of his sister-in-law, "When Willa went out today, where did you suppose her gone?"

"With Sir Nigel," Leonora said promptly. "Not to elope with him, of course, but she had mentioned to me some days ago that she was to visit some cousin or aunt of his with him, and asked me if I would go with her. I could not today, of course, and I was surprised that she had gone. I never guessed that she had this in mind, Adam; I truly believed that she was in love with you."

Ignoring the extraneous, Adam said curtly, "Where did this aunt live and what was her name?"

"What can it possibly matter?" said Lady Anne. "They never went there, you can depend upon it."

Adam calmly repeated his question and Leonora said, "I think Willa said it was in Cuckfield, or near it. I don't know that Willa ever mentioned the name to me, but I have something in my head that sounds like Collins or Conlan. Are you going after her, Adam? Oh, please bring her home if you can. She may have thought her fight with you last night desperate, but I am certain that it is not him that she cares for."

"I shall certainly go after her," Adam said, his voice grim.

Lady Anne gave a shriek. "You are not to be fighting a duel with him, Adam. I won't have it. What is to become of us if you get yourself killed? Mr. Gordon, you must go with him and prevent him from any rashness."

Stephen, acutely aware of his awkwardness in this most private family matter, said hastily, "I would be glad to be of service to you, my lord, in any way you would wish."

Adam sighed and smiled dourly. "If you can keep some peace in this house and a modicum of discretion while I am gone, I shall be greatly in your debt."

According Lady Anne only the briefest of bows, he went at once to his own chamber. He rang to have his racing curricle sent for again and a fresh team put to it, and then changed with a rapidity that astonished his valet. He sent for Barrow to wait on him while he dressed and ascertained from him the extent of the knowledge belowstairs and dispassionately discussed with him the means of squelching the gossip to keep it from penetrating beyond his house.

In the remarkable space of less than half an hour, he was once again on the road he had so recently traveled, and without so much as a groom for company.

∽13∾

Reluctantly Willa entered the inn with Sir Nigel and saw that the interior was not spacious. The taproom held only a few small tables, and though one or two doors to the opposite sides of the kitchens held the promise of leading into parlors, it was likely that these would be small and probably not comfortably furnished. But the place seemed clean enough and there was only a single patron in the taproom who had the appearance of being an honest farmer. Willa relaxed a bit and made no demur while Sir Nigel asked if there was a private parlor to be had.

The landlord led them to a back room with a small hearth, a single window, and a table that had seen better days. Willa sat in one of the room's two chairs. "I wonder what Mama and Leonora must be thinking," she said. "I hope they are not thinking that we have gone into a ditch."

Sir Nigel did not appear to share her concern. He shrugged slightly. "They are seasoned travelers and familiar with all the annoying mishaps that can befall one on the road; most are relatively harmless."

The landlord came back into the room at that moment and Sir Nigel at once began to order their dinner. Willa stared at him in astonishment and, as soon as the man had gone, said, "Why have you ordered more than wine and biscuits? We haven't the time to wait for a meal to be prepared, let alone to eat it!"

Sir Nigel only smiled at her anxiety. "Dear lady, if you are not peckish, I am. It will do us both more good to take the time for a bit of nourishment than to go on fainting with hunger when we must wait in any case."

"You may do so if you please," Willa said, her anger rising again, "but I mean to go on to Brighton, and at once."

"How shall you do that, my dear?" he asked with interest.

"There must be some vehicle to be had here that I may hire. I can drive, you know."

"I don't doubt it," he said amiably, "but you must remember that this is not the sort of place you are used to. There may be a cart, I suppose, but there is nothing to pull it, as our predicament proves. Content yourself to wait, my dear; there is really nothing else at all that you can do."

Willa could have cried with vexation, but she saw the truth of his words. He was determined, and she was captive to his determination. Resisting the temptation to pout, she simply lapsed into silence.

Dinner was plain, but plentiful, though Willa ate almost none of it. Sir Nigel commented on her want of appetite, but could not induce her to relax and enjoy the meal, so he did so himself, making no haste at all and putting her even more on the fret.

After what seemed an interminable time, he finished his meal and rang for the landlord to remove the covers. Willa breathed a sigh of relief, but it quickly turned to a gasp of indignation as he asked the landlord if there was any port to be had.

"Port!" Willa said, fairly shouting the word. "This is outside of enough! Take me home at once, if you please."

Sir Nigel took in a long breath and let it out again.

There was a smile of sorts on his lips, but a mocking light in his eyes. "But you see, my dear, I do not please."

Willa caught her breath, suspicion dawning in her eyes. He went on, "I have hesitated to tell you, but I fear the axle of the carriage is cracked. It would be most foolhardy to try to make it to Brighton before it is repaired. I fear that will not be possible before morning."

Willa stared at him in disbelief. Despite evidence to the contrary, she had never wished to think poorly of Sir Nigel, but she could not avoid the truth now. "There is nothing wrong with the axle," she said with flat statement.

His smile widened. "No."

"You do not mean to drive me back to Brighton tonight."

"No."

"Was this your plan from the beginning?"

"But of course," he admitted, and added in a cajoling tone, "Why don't you have a bit of this excellent wine— surprisingly so—and make yourself as comfortable as you may? You will only feed your agitation if you keep glowering at me in that way and you may take my word for it that any scheming to escape my wicked clutches is utterly pointless. You don't even know where you are, do you? Perhaps you have guessed by now that any servants you find here, including the landlord, will be deaf and blind to your entreaties."

Willa believed him, but she could not give him the satisfaction of obeying him in even a small thing, and she turned away from him and got up to take an agitated turn about the small room.

"I knew about the cockfight in Horley and that Revis meant to attend and decided I could not find a better day for my plan," he said to her. "Did you enjoy meeting my aunt? That was a nice touch, was it not? Revis had an aunt for you to visit, and so did I. Perhaps it was too subtle."

"Is she your aunt?"

"Of course not," he replied almost impatiently. "She carried it off tolerably well, I think, though I doubt she ever heard of Sir Hammish before I told her of him a fortnight ago. She was once on the boards, you know, before she married Mr. Conklin and became respectable. Jane loves greasepaint, though, and keeps up her connections with the theater."

His mention of the theater made Willa recall the theatrical performance of Mrs. Petrie and Adam's comment that there was some sort of connection between her and Sir Nigel. "Is that where you came to know Isobella Petrie?" she asked waspishly.

"She is Jane Conklin's niece, actually," he said with a light laugh.

Willa rounded on him. "You sent her to me!" How abysmally stupid she had been; how insecure of herself that she could readily believe that Adam could so easily betray her. He had accused her of being so set on being right that she was determined to bring them to grief, and now she believed that his accusation was justified.

Sir Nigel bowed ironically. "You recognize my hand. I am honored." She turned her back on him again. "Actually," he continued, "my original plan was to give you such a disgust of Revis that you would fall into my waiting arms, but you are a stubborn woman, Willa. I daresay I set up your back with my original offer, though it was always flatteringly meant. And so, my dear, lovely prude, I do you the honor of complete honesty."

"If you will call me anything, call me a fool," Willa said wretchedly. "I should have known better than to trust you. Perhaps I did know better, for I had meant for Nora to come with us and I certainly would not have left the house if I had guessed that Lady Meering was not to be with us."

"I am a flexible man, my dear," he told her. "If you had

rought your sister, I should have played the scene out at ace value and come up with something else. Eventually I hould have had you, you know. I told you quite some ime ago that I meant to make you mine, and mistake me ot, I shall."

"By force," she said fiercely.

He inclined his head. "As you wish."

A chill ran through Willa; she knew that he meant it. "I lon't understand you. Why would you wish for me un-villing? Do you wish to revenge yourself upon me because would not accept you as my lover when you offered me arte blanche?"

"In part, dear girl, but it is much more than that. It is nostly as I have always said: I want you and I intend to aave you. Beginning this very night," he added with dis-inct menace in his voice.

Willa suppressed a shudder but crossed her arms before ner as if to hug herself for comfort. "I suppose you may ake me physically if you are set upon it," she said quietly, "but the only man I shall ever belong to is my husband."

"Literally speaking, that is true, but only for now. I ancy that after tonight the situation will change."

"I shall never want you of my free will," she rejoined, "and Adam would not abandon me to your connivance. When he discovers what you have done, he will make you account for this."

"I see I must disillusion you, fair lady," he said with a mile that was horrible to her. "When Revis discovers vhere you have gone, he will not rush to protect you. He vill believe that it is your choice. I had the foresight, you ee, to leave him a small note, making it quite clear to him hat I wrote at your behest. It explained 'our' intentions in erms that would curl the horns of the most complacent uckold. We will agree, I think, that he is not that. A roud man, Revis. I will say this in his favor."

Willa's heart sank. This was a nightmare indeed. She sa
down again wearily. Not only was there no hope fo
tonight, there was no hope for the future. "There is n
conquest in force," she said in a listless way.

"That is for me to decide. You ought not to be so se
against it. You may not want me now, but tomorrow may
be quite another matter."

Willa raised her chin with defiant pride. She woul
make him fight for the smallest caress. "I'll never come t
you willingly," she spat at him.

"A pity, but come to me you will." He rose languidl
from his chair and walked around the table to her. Sh
stiffened, following him with her eyes but remaining a
expressionless as she could, determined not to let him se
her fear of him. He reached a hand toward her and sh
slapped it away. But he only laughed at her. She knew sh
had to get away from him, even if just temporarily t
gather her scattered wits.

"I don't suppose you mean to ravish me here," she said
letting her disgust of him show in her voice. "There is
bedchamber, I presume?"

"Eager, are you, my dear? I told you you should com
about."

She did not bother to answer this. "It has been a lon
day and I am tired. I wish to refresh myself and wash of
some of the dirt of travel. If you have any decency at all
which I wonder at, you will allow me a bit of time b
myself for this."

"And give you the opportunity to escape through
window?" he asked perceptively. "I have already though
of that, you know. You will find the windows all shuttere
and locked. Nor should you think of locking me out of th
room." He pulled a key from a pocket. "The only one, m
dear, and I shall use it from the inside. Go if you like.
shall give you a quarter-hour while I enjoy mine host's

excellent wine." He stood a little away from her and Willa got up quickly.

"You will find the chamber of our pleasures the first at the top of the stairs to your left. The other rooms are safely locked."

Willa went up the stairs quickly and, ignoring his words, tried all the doors. Only the one he told her of opened. It was also true that the window in that room was shuttered and locked. There would be no escape from there. Standing at the top of the stairs, she looked down into the empty taproom and saw that he had left the door to the parlor open. It stood between her and the outside door and she did not think it possible that she could pass it without his detection; in any case, he was so thorough that she supposed he had locked the door to the courtyard as well.

She went back into the bedchamber where a fire was already lit. She lit a candle from this and at once began a search of the room. Tepid water sat in a bowl on a high chest and beside it lay several towels, but beyond this she could find not another single thing in the room but the furniture and the hangings.

Willa was not sure what she was looking for, but she was determined to find some means of defending herself against her kidnapper. Every drawer in the chest was empty, but in despair she ran her hand along the bottom and back of each. In the third drawer her hopes were realized better than she had dared to hope. It was only a letter opener of greatly tarnished brass. Its point was not sharp and there was no great cutting edge to the blade, but it would do. He might do his worst, but he would not come away unscathed.

She concealed her weapon in the folds of her carriage dress and sat down on the bed to await her attacker, carefully arranging her skirts about her so that she would have quick access to her defense as soon as she should need it.

Self-condemnation for her gullibility, which had brought her to this, was as fruitless as conjecture for her future, so she tried to keep her mind on what she would do when he came to her. She had sat there only a minute or two when she heard a noise that made her heart beat faster. Horses were approaching the inn at a pace that must be reckless for the condition of the road. Though she had no real hope of it happening, she willed it to turn into the courtyard. To her astonishment, it did, and came to a halt almost exactly beneath her window. Because of the locked shutters, she could not look out to see the face of the person she already thought of as her rescuer, so she rushed into the hall. At the top of the stair she halted and waited for the knock at the door, wondering if it would be answered and, if it were not, what the newcomer would do.

But the door to the courtyard was not locked as she had supposed, and it opened with the squeal of unoiled hinges. Sir Nigel had come to stand in the doorway of the parlor, as intent as she on seeing who had arrived.

Beyond hope, beyond belief, it was Adam. Sir Nigel's lounging posture in the doorway became straight and she heard him mutter a curse.

Adam's face looked like it was carved in rock. "Where is she?" he asked in a voice of steel.

Sir Nigel smiled slowly. "In our bedchamber, where I left her," he said deliberately.

Adam's hand balled into a fist, and in the space of a moment Sir Nigel was on the floor in front of him, bleeding from the corner of his mouth.

Recovering from her shock at seeing him, Willa rushed down the stairs with enough airiness to do Leonora credit and fairly flung herself into her husband's arms. She clearly startled him, but he did not push her away as she had

alf-feared. He looked her up and down rather quickly.
Are you well?"

"She is ecstatic," said Sir Nigel, who had picked himself
up and was tending to his wound with his handkerchief.

"He is lying, Adam," she said with quiet dignity. "I
ave taken no harm of him. Please believe that."

But Adam did not appear to be heeding her. He stared
at Allerton in a piercing way, and when he addressed her,
his eyes never left Sir Nigel's face. "Go back upstairs and
wait, Willa. We shall be leaving very shortly."

"Are you certain of that, my lord?" Sir Nigel said with
cool menace.

"Yes."

Willa felt a chill of apprehension. She was scarcely
surprised when she saw Adam pull a long thin case from
the folds of his drab coat where he had concealed it. She
recognized it at once: a prime set of dueling pistols that he
had once shown to her and mentioned he had had made to
his order by Manton.

"Dear God, Adam, no!"

He turned sharply, as if surprised to still find her there.
"Go upstairs, Willa." This time it was a command.

"You can't duel in this place," she said, shocked. "You
don't even have seconds. What if he should kill you?" she
added with rising alarm.

At last his eyes held hers. "Very touching, my love. Is
your concern for me or yourself? You need not have any. I
am a very competent shot."

His expression and his tone were implacable. She knew
he would do this whatever she might say.

"She is right, Revis," said Sir Nigel, who had resumed
his casual pose. "It is too irregular. In any case, there is no
need to fight. You may have her back if you wish; I am
done with her."

Adam's eyes narrowed to mere slits. "It is either this or

I take my horsewhip to you, Allerton. You may have th
choice."

A martial light came into Sir Nigel's eyes. He bowe
stiffly and went into the room. Adam followed him an
the door was closed with a snap behind him, leaving Will
alone in the taproom.

If she could not stop the fight, she did not wish to watc
it. She did not think she could bear it if the worst shoul
happen. She walked sightlessly over to one of the table
but could not bring herself to sit placidly and await he
fate. Every muscle was tense and waiting; without realiz
ing it, she held her breath. The silence was so deafenin
that when she finally heard the sound she waited for, i
seemed a small thing.

She could not wait to see which man would open th
door and she ran over to it, wrenching it open. There wa
a stench of gunpowder in the room, but both men stoo
before her. Adam's back was to her, but he turned at he
entrance. She thought his face had lost some of its hardness

Impossible to think that either had deloped in this situa
tion, and she had fully expected to find one of them on th
floor with his life's blood oozing away. Her eyes ques
tioned Adam, but he only said, "Have you your reticule
Willa? We shall be leaving now, for I do not wish to caus
your mother and Nora any more anxiety than is necessary."

Willa could only nod at this commonplace speech, s
filled was the scene with anticlimax. Even Sir Nigel smile
in a rather pleasant way as he walked over to Adam an
handed him the other gun, butt first.

"The rubber is yours, my lord," he said easily. "If yo
wish to be a generous winner, you will send word to m
valet to have him come to me here with any damne
sawbones he can get on short notice."

One hand was in his coat, and when he pulled it out
there was blood on his fingers. It was only then that Will

noticed the hole in his coat and realized that he had been shot.

"You may consider it done," Adam said briskly. "But you would oblige me if you would have the landlord of this hole fix you a pad to staunch the blood. I've no wish to be inconvenienced for the killing of you."

Sir Nigel laughed softly. "Do you imply that you spared me deliberately? Well, perhaps you did. In your place I should have certainly shot to kill. I think we are even now."

For the first time Adam smiled. "Do you? I consider myself to be considerably up on you, Allerton. You have been chastised, but have done me no lasting harm."

"No?"

"No." He held out his hand to Willa to come to his side, and she took his arm.

"What makes you so sure?"

"A thorough knowledge of my wife," he replied succinctly. He picked up the case with the guns, which he had replaced. "If you think to resume this game," he said softly, "be sure of this. Next time I *shall* kill you."

With these parting words, he led Willa from the inn to his curricle, which was being held by the same ostler who had tended Sir Nigel's carriage. Willa saw a generous coin slip into the man's hand from Adam's, and knew why he had switched his loyalties.

As Adam gathered up the reins, Willa said, "Adam, I must tell you—"

"Not now," he interrupted, not angrily, but firmly enough to make her obedient.

They exchanged not another word the entire distance to the Marine Parade. It was a most uncomfortable trip in the dark and in an open carriage, but Willa, with a thousand thoughts rampaging through her head, scarcely noticed the discomforts. She wondered what she would face when she returned home, the anxieties and reproaches of her mother and sister, no doubt, but what concerned her most was that there would be more of this steely coldness from Adam, whose love for her she was certain she had stupidly destroyed.

Glad to be home but heavy in spirit, Willa entered the front hall to be greeted with a quick embrace from her sister. A little behind her stood Stephen, who gave her a smile that told her all she needed to know about his presence there. As Leonora escorted Willa up the stairs, she confided in her that Lady Anne had at last come to think of her Stephen as a welcome suitor for her hand.

Lady Anne was still preserving a picture of prostrate elegance, but she had moved to the lounge in the corner of her room, content to let her delicacy be stated by her reclining position and a wonderfully wrought dressing gown. Upon seeing Willa enter the room with Leonora, she gave a small shriek of delighted relief and held out her arms for Willa to embrace her. Willa went to her at once.

"Were I not so pleased to see you, my love," Lady Anne said with some severity, "I should tell you that you are a wicked, wicked girl to go off in such a way. No doubt you have been deceived in Nigel just as I have been all these years. You must forget him, of course. Adam is a sensible man; if you are dutiful and present yourself with propriety from now on, no doubt he will agree not to put you aside." Then, calling Stephen by his given name, she asked him to fetch her a bit of brandy to calm her nerves.

This mode of address, plus Stephen's accepted presence in a private family situation, made it clear to Willa that for Leonora, at least, all was to end in happiness. Chiding herself for self-pity, she said to her mother, "It is not as you think, Mama. I did not go with Sir Nigel willingly, but I am ashamed to admit that I was quite easy to deceive; I never guessed his intentions. I don't know what the note he left said, but I can well guess. It was all lies."

Lady Anne seemed vastly relieved, but Leonora was curious. "How did you find Willa, Adam?"

Adam had come into the room without Willa being aware of him, and when she followed her sister's gaze to where he sat slouched wearily in an armchair near the hearth, she was disconcerted to find him watching her. But he then transferred his regard to Leonora. "It was not even as difficult as I feared it would be. I will save you the tedious details, but I discovered almost by accident at the Red Lion at Hand Cross, where I went when Allerton's trail grew cold in Cuckfield, that the aunt's name was not Collins but Conklin, as in Jane Conklin, once of Covent Garden fame. She was easy enough to find and not so very difficult to persuade that it was in her best interest to reassess her loyalties. She did not know for certain where he had taken Willa, but she knew of a place on a back road into Brighton where he sometimes took a light-o'-love when he wanted complete privacy. It was there that I found them."

Leonora was wide-eyed and even Lady Anne and Stephen were rapt in his words. "You didn't call him out, did you, Adam?" Leonora asked.

"Suffice it to say that my honor is satisfied."

Lady Anne gasped. "Never say you have killed him!"

"I trust not," Adam said, his voice falling into a familiar drawl. "You need not be concerned for him, but neither do I think the world will see much of him for a time."

"I intend never to see him again," Lady Anne said positively.

Feeling weary to the point of near fainting, Willa begged to be allowed to go to her room to change and wash, and her mother and sister were at once all solicitousness. Leonora escorted her to her room, but at Willa's assurance that she needed no support, gladly returned to be with her Stephen.

When Willa was finally washed and changed into a pale-lavender silk nightdress and matching dressing gown, she knew that she could no longer put off the inevitable interview with her husband. She was not at all secure about what she should say to him.

She had been such a fool; it was even beyond foolishness. She had deliberately believed badly of him because of her own vulnerability and a self-defeating determination to prove that her original judgment of them as ill suited to each other was correct. She had been so set on the idea that her marriage must fail that at the first sign of discord she was ready to discard the whole.

If Sir Nigel had sent Mrs. Petrie to her, then nothing that woman had said could be given credence. Adam had told her he was faithful to her, and now, too late, she must believe him. If she had found it so hard to believe in him, what must he think of her now? What must he have thought as he read Sir Nigel's note when there was her own behavior in encouraging Sir Nigel to defy him to weigh as evidence against her?

Yet he had come after her. Was it only his pride and his honor that had made him risk his life to bring her back to him? It was a bleak thought, but to set against it was his assertion to Sir Nigel that he had never believed her false to him. She prayed that he had not just said that for Sir Nigel's benefit.

Though her body ached with tiredness and her mind felt fuzzy and dull with all the anxieties and emotions that had bombarded it since the night before, she knew she did not want to spend the night with her fate unknown. When Doakes left her, she took her courage in both hands and went to their adjoining door, intending to just open it so that he could not gainsay her if he did not wish to speak with her still. But before she could touch the handle, the door opened from the other side and Adam stood before her framed in the doorway.

"I've come to bid you good night," he said with an ease she could envy, "and to see that you are well. You've had an interesting twenty-four hours."

"As have we all," she said with some feeling. She saw that he too had washed and changed, but he was dressed for the street.

He saw her speculative look and said, "I shall go to Raggets for an hour or two tonight. I think it would be best if I put in an appearance in public. It would go a long way, I think, to scotch any rumors if it was known that I was seen about in a casual way."

She dropped her eyes from his. "I can imagine what you must have thought when you read Sir Nigel's letter. You have gone to great lengths to protect me and my name."

"You are my wife."

"But I think now that it must be you who is sorry for the bargain you have made," she said. "Forgive me, Adam. But only for being a fool. I swear to you with all of my heart that Nigel was never anything to me at all."

For a moment he did not answer. Then he cupped her chin in his hand and raised her head so that she had to look at him. "If there is to be harmony between us, we must understand each other. I am sorry to say that I have discovered in myself a degree of possessiveness that I once assured you would never mar our relationship. I've no wish to take from you your freedom or independence, but you have taken it to the limit, Willa. I want my wife to be a woman of spirit and independence, but she must also be exclusive. Horns are not an appendage that I shall wear with complaisance."

His eyes told her nothing, but she feared that by his words he did think that there had been more between her and

Sir Nigel than there was. He let her go, but she still looked up at him. "I prided myself on my discernment, but I have been as naïve as any schoolroom miss. I knew what Nigel could be, but I thought I was clever enough to manage you both. I should not be surprised that I came a cropper."

He smiled slightly. "We have both made mistakes," he said handsomely. "Let us agree that we have both been unwise. I am willing to begin again if you are. We will go to bed this night, and tomorrow, if you agree, begin again on new terms."

This was sweeping out the past indeed. Tears welled into her eyes. "I love you, Adam," she said hoarsely. "Please say that I haven't destroyed all chance of its return." Before he could even reply, she was overcome with sobs, held back through so much this day.

He embraced her lightly. "I don't believe I have yet said how I feel," he said very softly.

She stemmed her emotion long enough to look up at him, and what she saw in his eyes turned her weeping into cries of joy. He let her weep on his impeccable coat by Weston, brushing his lips against her ear and throat and whispering sweet things that told her he loved her beyond reason.

When at last Willa had some control of herself, she moved a little away from him and saw that his eyes were far from dry as well. How impossible to think of it; how touching to realize that this man, who was always so in command of himself, should weep for love of her! He bent his head and kissed her tenderly, and she knew that she had after all made the match of discernment that she had promised herself and her father she would.

After a little time had passed in this happy occupation, she said, "If you are going to Raggets, you had best be about it. It is well after midnight, I think."

He sighed and removed the pearl stickpin from his cravat in a very deliberate way. "I believe I shall contrive to think of another way to answer any gossip should it arise from the servants' chatter."

"You might pay them triple wages for the quarter," she suggested, watching with fascination as he stripped himself of his cravat. "But then they might be suspicious at such largess," she continued, "and think worse things than really happened."

"I think I shall let them think what they will," he said loftily. "When the world observes us unfashionably loving toward each other, they shan't believe a word of what is said."

Willa gave him a severe look and walked over to the bed to sit on the edge. "You are sanguine, my lord," she said. "Mama had a letter only yesterday from Sir Walter Scott saying that he shall be visiting friends in Worthing soon and expects to come to Brighton to pay us a visit. If he suspected any indecorum in our behavior, he would be bound to cut us."

"A fate not to be thought of!"

"You mock me, sir," she said reprovingly as she stood to remove her dressing gown. "But you must promise upon your honor not to offer to take him to any cockfights."

"Done," he agreed, and went over to her. "I fear it is more likely George Byron we shall have on our doorstep if Nora has Stephen. He will feel not only the pull of intellect, but may also regard us as kin. You must be sure to instruct Cook to keep an adequate supply of boiled potatoes and vinegar on hand."

She could not prevent her smile. "And I shall lay in an adequate supply of curl papers as well," she said, and laughed.

"Unkind. I thought you rather liked him." He took the silk dressing gown from her hands and tossed it onto a nearby chair. "I wonder you did not set your cap at him," he said speculatively as he lightly embraced her. "His manners may be a bit odd at times, but he is a very pretty fellow."

"I am not in his style. He prefers older women, I am told."

"Lamentable taste."

She wrapped her arms about his neck and said into his ear, "I think you are prettier."

He laughed in his throat. "You are a woman of rare discernment," he said, and took her with his lips. Still entwined, they came down together on the goose-down bed, and whatever differences still lay between them were consigned to perdition, cast unheeded to the floor with the rest of their garments.

About the Author

Originally from Pennsylvania, Elizabeth Hewitt lives in New Jersey with her husband, Jim, and her dog, named Maxim after a famous romantic hero. She enjoys reading history and is a fervent Anglophile. Music is also an important part of her life; she studies voice and sings with her church choir and with the New Jersey Choral Society. MARRIAGE BY CONSENT was written to a background of baroque music, as were her previous novels for Signet's Regency line.